FLIGHT OF BLACK SWANS

FLIGHT OF
BLACK SWANS

Laura Fish

Duckworth

First published in 1995 by
Gerald Duckworth & Co. Ltd.
The Old Piano Factory
48 Hoxton Square, London N1 6PB
Tel: 0171 729 5986
Fax: 0171 729 0015

p. 76: 'Everything that Glitters (is not Gold)', by Bob McDill
and Dan Seals © 1985 Polygram Music Ltd and Pink Pig Music.
Reproduced by permission of the publishers.

p. 102: 'While the Damper Cooks', by Slim Dusty © Slim Dusty
Enterprises Ltd. Reproduced by permission of the publisher.

pp. 115-16: 'City Kind of Girl' by Robert Gundry © 1986
WB Music Corp. and Amachrist Music, USA. Reproduced by
permission of International Music Publications Ltd.

A catalogue record for this book is available
from the British Library

ISBN 0 7156 2645 0

This novel is a work of fiction. Names, characters, places and incidents
are either the product of the author's imagination or are used fictitiously and
any resemblance to actual persons, living or dead, is entirely coincidental.

Typeset by Ray Davies
Printed in Great Britain by
Redwood Books Ltd, Trowbridge

Acknowledgments

The author wishes to thank those who have given their guidance and support and apologise for any unintentional breaches of trust. Special thanks are to Stephen Rodber, Michael Croucher, Jane McCallan, Sue Wolstenholm, June Pederson, David Mowaljarlai, Peter Bibby, Angela Mbuli, Leith Bell, The Sir Robert Menzies Centre for Australian Studies in London, family, and friends in the Tamar Valley, Perth and the Kimberley, without whom this book would not have been written.

To Colin and Charlie

Glossary of Terms

S LINGING HIS RIFLE on the cushioned seat behind, he sang
from an old man's heart. A plaintive drone, strange and
stirring, swallowed in the mountain's belly. Although the land
had been taken from him, he belonged to it forever. Gnarled
fingers like the boab's branches; plum cheeks singed ashen; fur-
rowed brow rugged, scabrous; tousled hair thinned, feathery as
wind-brushed wisps of silky oil grass; his virtue a stubborn humility laurelled with pride spiky as spinifex. His perennial soul was
singing back creation.

The elder took her to the top of a hill from which they could
see his country spread before them – blues, reds, greens, magnifi-
cent and still in heat; told her how, in his youth, young men
wrestled with crocodile.

"I gotta pick up my son, take you to John Spires'. If 'e got work
you can stay there. You got yer things, we might shoot bush
turkey on the way, eh. If John got no work I'll give High Rocky a
call, new manager there, 'e sacked that Looma mob. I'll take my
son to another camp, drive back to Derby, keep the turkey for
tucker. Carl, 'e'll come 'n' pick you up."

Passing trucks overflowed with brown arms waving, white
teeth smiling, trailing dust clouds, copper in the airstream. A
frill-necked lizard confronted the vehicle. There were no bush
turkey. The white world she had known – a dissembled apogee,

spinning, infringing, striving for identity. "Can't blame 'em, they got none yet," remarked Paddy, "we hardly seen any animals." The elder's voice told of his many wives and children. Dusk descended, bush turkey flocked; like old women haggling they jostled at the roadside. Paddy stopped the land cruiser, reaching for his gun, indicated that Susan should stay put. Stealthily he opened the door, edged round the bonnet sneaking, stalking at close range, surreptitious behind the fearless fowl; aimed, pulled, 'click', the barrel didn't fire. He tickled the trigger – suspense – a bullet rang out. The limping bird was only shot in a wing. Snatching at its tail feathers Paddy pounced, overthrew the massive turkey, grappling in quivering grasses wrung its neck; plucked the body, leaving head and entrails for dingo, warm carcass cleaned in the dam.

It was pitch dark when the land cruiser lost momentum, and the engine ceased disturbing the night. They had run out of fuel.

Straying into spinifex for a place to use as a latrine, sensing danger, Susan shone the torch on a death adder's arc, its puffy crescent mirrored the curved toe of her boot. Paddy laughed, amused at the thought of sucking venom from the girl's buttocks.

They hitched a lift to a cluster of caravans nestled in the valley. All the men were drunk, they had been mining. They filled the jerry and ferried them back.

"If we're the earth's children, at best those men are mother-fuckers," said Paddy, the wisdom of mountains grinning from his eyes as the miners' tail lights disappeared over the brow. Susan thought uneasily of the gaping shaft at the end of her garden in Cornwall. It wasn't until sunrise that they discovered the spare tank.

Susan heard a Land Rover hesitantly pull up outside the bungalow.

Carl Roberts had set off from High Rocky cattle station at

noon, using Susan as an excuse to collect his car and spend two drunken days at the Spinifex Inn. Daylight dwindled when he reached the outskirts of town, coolness crowned the end of a close day.

Carl stopped on the opposite side of the road. He must have been counting the lot numbers. Knowle Way, 992. His tall, lean, drink-sodden figure tramped up the front steps. He told her he'd return the following morning, early, with his own Cadillac.

Carl was late. Another listless morning passed for Susan and two more journeys into town on a bicycle.

It must have been after two o'clock. Susan was past the point of despair, seated on her rolled-up swag, feeling overheated in her only jeans, a favourite flowery blue cotton shirt, kept for best though rather faded, cotton socks and an already well-trodden pair of leather ankle boots. She was counting every torrid, hour-like minute when the door bell rang and there he was. He seemed to her an ageless cowboy slouched against the balcony post on his right forearm, left hand resting on his hip.

Carl exuded authenticity and grog, his creased face, seasoned and golden from a harsh sun, was drawn with time. Susan would never have guessed he was the station manager's father.

Carl studied the girl with sky-blue eyes. Susan was in her early twenties; female physique fit and slim, rich dark skin, a braid of black locks protruding from her stately Akubra; under the rim oval almond-brown eyes often looked away shyly. Carl cocked his head, tilted down his ten gallon hat and gave her his left hand; it felt like worn, crumpled leather.

"G'day. Sorry, bit late, lady. I'll help you with yer swag if I may."

"Yes, thanks."

Carl took a second look, Susan assumed this was because he had noticed her English accent.

They walked into the house. Susan was feeling vaguely grateful; a new person to learn. Then, as the realisation finally struck, excitement began to build. A dream had come true. She was going to work on a cattle station.

Carl was a gentleman, weighed down with the cumbersome swag and rucksack, he wouldn't hear of her carrying anything. The Cadillac was shiny and new looking, the boot neatly packed with eskis. Susan was impressed. Carl established himself in the driver's seat, Susan sat with her feet lost in a heap of Country and Western tapes, her head disappearing into a dream, a glimpse of Derby's ominous water tower, and they said farewell to town through slightly tinted glass.

Carl sped along the tarmac highway in the direction of Fitzroy. He was hopelessly drunk so any lingering fears of violation subsided as Susan resigned herself to a rapid death, accepting that when the worst happened, the cause would be Carl's driving. Perhaps he sensed her fear, but instead of decreasing speed, offered her a beer and yarned about High Rocky. Carl warned that the manager, Bill, who had recently taken over, could be a cruel man, even though he said so himself, explaining how he failed to see why his boy had turned out as he had. Carl had tried to be good to him. Manners don't cost. He guessed some people turn out hard no matter what you do. The description of his son grew to ogre-like proportions. Carl only planned to stay at High Rocky for a few more weeks, days even, then he'd head back to Queensland where he'd spent most of his droving days. He wanted to retire, but he also wanted someone to go with him, perhaps Susan was interested in going too. He hoped she'd be okay at High Rocky, that the bad language wouldn't offend.

Susan said, "All I want is to work with the horses and cattle." This lit a spark in Carl and Susan's passion was rekindled by the brief memoirs of a drover.

Carl turned a tape in the machine. "Now the cattle are mustered by chopper, then on horseback and transported to Port Hedland by road train. They get knocked about by the truckin', an' the meat's a bit bruised, but it's faster this way." Carl could

12

remember the days when they drove cattle with horses all the way from High Rocky to Derby jetty before shipping them to the Far East. He got a good price for them then. They were on the old cattle trail now. In the past he used to stop at night for the cattle to feed.

The tape finished. Carl said, "You know 'The Moon In The Kimberley'? Brilliant song that is." He turned the tape. "Well, I could've sworn it was the first track on this side. You wait, it'll be after this one."

So they waited.

"Well, I could've sworn it was the next one, y'know. You'll love it when you hear it, I jus' know you will."

They waited again. He pressed fast forward. "It's on this tape, I know, I've heard it an' I'll find it. You sure you don't know it? P'rhaps it's the last track. Yeah, me'be. You're really gonna like this one when you hear it." Fast forward, play, rewind, turn the tape again, play, fast forward. "I'll find that track if it's the last thing I do." He never did though. Carl would still be searching for "The Moon In The Kimberley" when the time came for him to leave High Rocky and Susan never heard it.

"You wanna beer? You sure?"

Susan nodded. Carl slowed the car, straying off the road into dust. He got out, went to the Cadillac's boot, selected three cans from an eski and returned with his clanking treasure. He offered Susan one again. The interior was getting stuffy, she didn't want to drink. Giving a surprised shrug, Carl carefully positioned two cans amongst the tapes lagging her feet, opening the third with a gracious air. An inert beery odour topped the vehicle up as Carl filled himself.

They set off again, resuming the high speed, whirling past the monotonous scrubby bush enduring the route. Carl drove even faster than before. He looked so comfortable.

"One helluva lotta black fellas die on this highway, y'know. One died th'other day. Y'know what happens?"

13

Susan looked at him thoughtfully. "No, I don't."

"They get real drunk, lie on the bitumen to 'ave a sleep, you see. This one lay flat across this highway in the dark an' some yute jus' goes straight over 'im. Them black fellas get drunk an' them jus' lie in the highway." Carl spoke chirpily and with renewed vigour, smiling at Susan with a twinkle in his eye as he swigged and appraised with the can in his hand. "Bump! Right over that black fella an' the yute never stopped." Carl's head enthusiastically endorsed his words, eyes brimming with beer. "Guess the poor bugger never noticed when that black fella was squashed right into the highway."

Susan's stomach turned. She wondered whether Carl would have felt the bump. When he described it she could.

There was a tedious ritual: Carl would fumble for a tape with his left hand, clutch a can in his right, claw the steering wheel with one finger, while swerving precariously in the middle of the road. Susan was amazed that he kept on the highway; her feet kept reaching for an imaginary brake pedal.

Carl found a desired cassette with which to feed the machine. Initiating another can, he sniggered. "Poor ol' black fella, eh?" Susan leant her head against the car window.

When she awoke the scenery had not changed; still that thick, low-lying bush.

"We turn off somewhere round 'ere," said Carl, mercifully reducing velocity, "unless yous wanna come back t'Queensland with me. We could go right on there now."

Susan forced a reticent smile to thank him but "No," and they veered right, off tarmac on to a broad gravel track, well textured with pot-holes. Carl steadied the car. He was tiring too.

The fitful track meandered, narrowing as they left dense scrub for open landscape. Comely dome-shaped mounds rose unexpectedly, their soft green, grassy banks feathered with golden spinifex. Haphazard boabs plumped the slopes and in the distance was a hazy range of voluptuous indigo mountains.

"There's an Aboriginal settlement near 'ere," said Carl. "A station community called Looma. We employ a handful of 'em. All the ringers on the stock camp at High Rocky used t'come from there, but they've mostly left now. There's been many changes. Bill musters from the air a lot – didn't see eye to eye with those boys so they walked out. Didn't like the way 'e mouths much either. Bill's saving grace is that he treats all them ringers the same, black or white, none are spared his language," chuckled Carl, unaware of the extent of his son's injustices, "so there's jus' two Aboriginal boys now an' a half-caste from Derby – 'e's head stockman. Davie. You'll be in his camp I guess. Davie's a bit of a buffoon, could be 'cos he's used to bein' treated as one, but I wouldn't have thought he'd lay a finger on a lady – not 'less she wanted him to, eh? There's a big store in the community. You might go down there with them boys one day. High Rocky's at the foot o' them blue mountains." He indicated with his head. "That's where we're goin'. Not far now. You all right, lady? You're real quiet."

Susan smiled at him politely. The road tacked, falling into a wide, parched river bed, the scarps clenched with talon-like roots of willowy trees. Carl told Susan how the creek had burst its banks in the wet and flooded the country right the way to High Rocky. As they hit shale in the heart of the cleavage, he decelerated, graunched the gears and stalled.

"This creek's fulla crocs. You won't be swimmin' 'ere. They mustered the creek th'other day. Dangerous that was. Too many trees. Some o' them boys was injured real bad. It's a good job you weren't working that day, eh?" Carl twiddled the key in the ignition, the Cadillac started, the tyres carved up a steep incline, zigzagging back to the track. There were a couple of gates for Susan to open, then they passed the first ramshackle outhouses, sheds and workshops of High Rocky. Carl pointed out the depressed kitchen block and bunk-house to the right, his bungalow opposite and a brief building he said the Canadian manager lived in. The track divided. On the island was a store. Carl took the left fork to pull up in the shade of the main station house porch. The drover looked exhausted. He got out and opened the door for Susan. She got out stiffly, blinking wide-eyed in sunlight, gathered her belongings, resting them against the whitewashed wall of the station house. Carl glanced at the girl. Disappointment. Who would go back north with him? And walked inside.

Slumped on her swag, Susan took in the surroundings. Across the yard to the left stood a giant metal frame supporting a water drum, behind it was a stable block, to the right of the block the track they had come on continued, sweeping round to yellow plain, stretching to the brumey horizon. Adjacent to the homestead were two oily-dark wooden sheds, housing a generator, a stripped-down Toyota pick-up and tools. A gap, more plain, a couple of long, battered caravans, one with a chained sleeping dog, glued to shade. Then the buildings Carl had pointed out: the flat-roofed bunk-house, the separate kitchen, wash and laundry room.

A black horse grazed in a square of sun-bleached paddock, plain again, windless heat, and a beautiful sky-blue sky. Susan loved the sky but her excitement transformed to fatigue. She was getting flu.

The housekeeper, Shelley, a lubberly white Australian in her mid-twenties, welcomed her into the homestead. Shelley was quite overjoyed to have a female to fuss for and busied herself with a hobby of trivialities. She wore a green T-shirt with matching thongs, her berry-blotched legs blazed and failed her sketchy shorts. They passed through a spacious modern kitchen where a black-faced microwave slept on well-wiped sideboards; through the dining room and outside to a narrow, rectangular rear porch, whose shade they sat under on deck chairs while Shelley chatted about fainting in the heat and panted.

Rotating sprinklers refreshed the pleasing lawn before them, the garden fence was complemented with scarlet and white

16

flowers. Susan thought she could have been anywhere in the relics of England's equatorial empire.

Bill's wife and the children were away in Broome for the week, everyone else was out working. Shelley said she would be happy for Susan to stay in her house. "I think it might be easier for you that way."

"Thank you for the offer," said Susan. "How long have you been at High Rocky?"

"Near on one year by the rains. The place used to be called Kakinpala, or summin', then Myroodah, Bill Roberts called it High Rocky when he came. Folks here keep changing place names."

A door slammed. Bill Roberts' colossal stature towered over the women. His voice boomed.

"G'day." Susan smiled weakly. The housekeeper jumped to her feet. "You bin lookin' after 'er? Well, take the girl to the bunk-house, she may as well settle in now as that's where she'll be livin'. There's plenty of rooms she can choose from. I've got work to do in my office, I'll 'ave lunch there, Shelley."

Bill Roberts returned to his office. Shelley went quiet, he had spoiled something inside her. Susan collected her belongings, Shelley led the way to the bunk-house leaving Susan outside. Their relationship ended as abruptly as it had begun.

In the middle of the bunk-house was a metal-framed door roughly coated with green aluminium gauze to keep flies out; the door opened into a corridor room fronted by glassless windows, also veiled in gauze. A wire bed with no mattress was situated at one end, at the other a pregnant suitcase spewed shirt-sleeves on to the neglected, red tile floor. Before Susan were six doors, a few of which were open. A sweet, sweaty, soapy smell was stale in the air; to her right, through the first door, she could see the shower.

"Hi there. G'day. Pleased to meet you." It was the Canadian manager (his accent was unmistakable). "I hear you've been givin' ol' Carl a good time. Yous wanna watch yerself 'round 'ere, young lady." He laughed. "Yous wanna watch these men 'ere too. Any trouble an' you come 'n' tell me. I'll take care of you an' if you want my opinion, you shouldn't be kippin' out 'ere with the boys." He laughed again. He stared at Susan curiously, as people sometimes did. She was used to being the odd one out. "They say you're a Pom – that true, is it? Never seen a Pom like you before." He wanted to know all about her: where she was really from, what she did there, what she had been doing in Australia, why she was at High Rocky. Susan took an instant dislike to him and kept words to a minimum. As he talked they toured the dank washrooms and gloomy laundry where cockroaches scuttled under a washing machine. There was an area at the back with a horizontal roof of woven wattle supported by spindly poles, through which they looked out on to shimmering grassland. Here a network of lines had been strung for drying washing. He showed her the drab kitchen-diner, sparsely furnished with chairs and a huge table, painted black, smeared in cruddy egg yolk and grime. The cooking area, cheerless compared with the station house kitchen, and even more stark, at a glance seemed relatively clean. In one corner a party of ants swarmed on the floor tiles below cool metal sideboards. Above the double sink and drainer was the only window, like the ones in the bunk-house, obscured by gauze.

The Canadian was only gone a few minutes. Susan didn't remember his name. He'd said he'd go find Davie. She stood drowsily in partial darkness, focusing abstractedly on ants as the flu symptoms triumphed.

Two men's feet softly thudded on dust.

"Hey Davie, meet my new lady." The Canadian manager's voice was strident as they entered. "Now watch yerself with Davie, 'e's gonna be yer new boss. I'll see yous around."

There was a long silence in the murky mango half-light, broken by Davie's husky, hesitant voice.

"Don't be 'fraid. You right, you 'ad a feed? Gotta eat. Make

18

you strong." His pitch, unusually cautious and abrupt, qualified the ruffled yellow-ochre hair, fallow as the plain; dusty, tempered, embrowned face, unshaven jaw, shirt unbuttoned to the belt, strapping chest with golden hairs and ample stomach billowing over trouser top. The stockman wore the mealy, malty aroma of horses; his overalls were soiled from the red earth corral.

"Don't be scared now. You'll be right 'ere, we'll look after you. Si' down." Davie gestured towards the black table. "Make yerself at 'ome. I'll cook you a feed." It was as though there was a light behind those volatile violet-blue eyes profoundly penetrating the darkness. Davie looked past Susan. A week went by before he looked directly at her. She respected the man for that.

Davie washed his hands, salted and fried a slab of beef, heated a can of green beans and made sweet tea with powdered milk. Then he sat with Susan at the dirt-encrusted table while she chewed like a nervous cat.

The few words Davie spoke were attentive. "I know you, see, seen you round Derby. Don't be 'fraid now. 'Elp yourself to tucker, plenty tucker 'ere. You'll be right. You'll see. Today you rest." He paused. "If you need any clothes you can 'ave some o' mine." Each sentence was short and to the point. Susan had never seen, or heard, anyone like Davie. She felt instinctively drawn.

The bunk-house, a filthy shower and toilet at one end, the row of bedrooms, each with a dusty wardrobe or free-standing cupboard, the scummy wash area, the dingy stockmen's kitchen – this was their domain. Although he left her alone to rest, Susan was aware of Davie's enigmatic presence all afternoon.

The station, situated half-way between Derby and Fitzroy Crossing, four or five kilometres from the Fitzroy River on the northern side, covered nearly two thousand square kilometres and felt miles from anywhere. In the last year only five inches of rain had fallen. It showed.

That evening the bunk-house was deserted, the ringers were at stock camp for a month. There was a hollow ambience.

In front of the kitchen two men slumbered as the sun set behind a plinthed porch. The "boys" Carl had referred to were grown men; they remained motionless when Davie introduced Susan. "Pete, Rikki, get up. Hey, I'm talkin' to you." They stretched, peering through tangled curls. "You be good to 'er, we gotta look after 'er, see." Davie coaxed them to stand and shake hands, which they did, saucer eyes evasive. "That's Pete 'n' Rikki, they right. You need anythin' you ask me, Pete or Rikki. I'm yer boss, see," reinforced Davie. "I'm 'ead stockman 'round 'ere."

Susan chose the middle bedroom. Outlandishly obstructing her doorway, Davie unrolled his swag beside the suitcase. Perhaps he was trying to be protective, he may have had other ideas.

It was a long night. Davie reduplicated banal smoke rings in the rustic corridor. Susan was painfully conscious of any noise she made and the weakness from flu.

A woman in Derby had warned her to always remain clothed in bed, no matter how close the night air, saying that a popular joke was to catch a python and put it on your face when you are sleeping: as you jump up from the shock of the snake, the men can see your nakedness. (She reassured Susan that python are not poisonous, but they can grow to over fifteen feet long and may bite if alarmed.) For the first time since arriving at the cattle station, Susan wondered what on earth she was doing there. Paddy, the elder, had bestowed plenty of advice: wondering how much was fantasy, Susan shuddered when she recalled his last words. "Take care at High Rocky. Men out 'ere can 'ave their way with a girl. If they turn bad, leave, you'll get hurt, but sometimes there's no way out."

Davie's agitated voice summoned Susan, saying they had a long day ahead. In the cold morning air she showered, dressed, putting on yesterday's clothes, and stumbled from the bunk-house to the brightly lit kitchen block. Breakfast was eaten on white plates at the expansive black table. Susan gulped down sugary tea and a slice of white bread while Davie packed the tucker box for smoko and cut lunch: billy cans stained with smoke and caffeine, personalised enamel mugs, powdered milk, sugar, a tin of dusty tea, bread, and meat remnants from last night's feed.

A flat-faced buggy waited outside the bunk-house; it resembled a miniature version of an old army truck with its coat of olive green. Davie handed the girl a small, blue, quilted anorak; he called Pete and Rikki, who had retreated to their swags after breakfast, and they joined a tatty heap of saddles, bridles and grubby blankets on the floor of the open-back buggy. They all lurched forward when Davie started the vehicle with a burst of speed, hurtling round in a semicircle, creating floury clouds of dust. Pete opened the three gates they had to pass through before hitting the main mountain track. The buggy's suspension was lousy. It rattled and bounced as they weft through scrub. Susan felt feverish but the warm air dried the flu symptoms while she slept for most of the journey.

It must have been at least an hour before Davie pulled up in crimped clay alongside a fence line, prodding Susan.

"We gotta take cattle from the yard, drive 'em out for feed, we'll be tailin' 'em. I'll show you what to do. Horses 'ere, see, by that bore."

At first all Susan saw was mustard-coloured dirt and shrubs against a cloudless blue sky. Laden with saddles, hessian nosebags heavy with feed, bridles dragging in dust, the trio strode out to the horses. Susan stayed in the truck. She could not see the bore but she could see the horses now, grazing amongst dwarfed trees.

On day one Davie gave Susan a stock horse, an ageing piebald with no name. With a flicker of perplexed excitement, an inimitable expression, he pressed the reins into her hand, and said with open frankness, "A present. 'Ave it fer Christmas." Susan was thrilled. But the stockmen didn't seem to be very fond of their horses, or so she thought.

Davie rode a fine bay mare, reddish-brown in colour with a black mane and tail, a white blaze and a soft pinky muzzle. Pete, a grey roan. Rikki's was sleek and black.

Heat was upon them from the start. Rikki's black mare bucked on the way to pasture, throwing him on low-spread desert love grass with a dull thump. He rose from the wiry crushed mosaics in an indelicate reel of lewd language. The cattle moved easily, holding well on the pastoral plateau, grateful for a plentiful feed. The stockmen knew High Rocky like animals, each track, hollow, hill and the people like a well-thumbed book. Susan was an accomplished rider. As they rode around the herd, Davie pointed out simple landmarks to give her some bearings. If the range was ahead, the station was behind, the cattle yards near the blue canyon, the short cut to the homestead.

A hypnotic aroma wafted over the warmed grasses. They watched brown cattle sublimely grazing, mounted ringers dormant in the intensity of the sun. Pete, Rikki, Davie, all starkly set against golden spinifex blended with silvery slivers of oil grass, backed by stolid purple mountains and a pale blue shroud of sky. The hottest part of the day, still, like deepest night. No birdsong now. Who dares to move. Let peace, let harmony blossom, love of the land, clear colour pure, brought to life by brilliant sunlight. Feeling serene, Susan wished the wheel of time would stop turning, just once, for this panoramic scene to remain untouched, undisturbed.

At midday Davie boiled a billy to make tea. While they rested in tufts of spinifex, he asked Susan, "You bin travellin' long in Australia?"

"About three months."

"So what you come 'ere for, come lookin' fer swans?"

"Swans?" said Susan, mystified.

22

"Yeah, black swans. Lotta Poms come 'ere lookin' fer black swans, they tell me there's none back in England. Them swans're the emblem for Western Australia. But you won't find 'em 'ere, they're further south."

"Oh," said Susan, who had thought that a black swan was a contradiction in terms.

"So, what you come 'ere for?"

"I'm on a working holiday."

"What's that then?" Davie inclined his head.

Repeating the words "working holiday" to herself, Susan realised she wasn't sure what the phrase meant. "It's just a thing some people do," she mumbled.

The conversation was becoming ambiguous. Davie wanted to talk straight and get on with the girl. "An' you were born in England, were you?"

Susan replied awkwardly, "Yes." She went self-conscious saying this. "I was adopted, by a white family." Susan had been adopted from birth at a time when trans-racial adoption was deemed highly commendable in Britain. Susan was not an advocate for this way of thinking. Adoption, she reasoned, was disjunction enough without racial complications. She shyly looked up and away from Davie, and flicked at a tall stem of grass.

The stockman was embarrassed. His violet-blue eyes were averted and he clawed his scalp with gritty nails. Reaching for his pannikin he talked of his parents, how he'd lost their language. For missionary sermons he had no taste. Davie sipped sweet tea.

The afternoon drew nigh, dreamy cattle fanned wider, browsing in vivid green conkerberry and the dense shrubs that composed a perimeter to the pasture lands. Birds shot away like darting arrows as stockmen dogged the thirsty, restless cattle, driving them to a hillside shaded with wattle and eucalyptus, air filled with a fresh scent.

Rikki spent the best part of the afternoon running down Bill Roberts; Susan shared jokes and side glances as she and Rikki worked. It had been a perfect day. She thought this over, seated on a pole in the cattle yard, watching the sky alight around a fireball descending and the full moon buoyantly suspended. The piebald drowsed, his head idling beside her boots, the reins looped round a post.

Bill Roberts drove up in a white Toyota. Stopping the truck in milling dust, he urgently hollered from the window, "There's a cow out on the track, on the hillside there, near the station. Best go bring 'er in sharp."

The piebald was emoted by the prospect of a mission and paced the track with a new lease of life. Upon reaching a divide in the bush Susan held the pony back to a trot. The downward slope of the short cut was steep; the gelding stumbled, disorderly over boulders, Susan bracing her legs, slanted back in the saddle, pending each coltish tumble with taut stirrup leathers and her boots compressed on the irons. Scouring the country for the cow, she sighted it, loping along a ridge; beyond, microscopic cattle sporadically garnished a hill's breast. There was no point in driving the one heifer back, in this vicinity it would be more expedient to round up all the stray cattle in the enclosure at the station turkey.

The sky darkened. The temperature dropped. Keeping the piebald to a narrowing path, Susan cantered the hillocky rise. It was arduous heeling the awkward cow. Half running, half stumbling, they verged impeding highland shrubs and traced a dusky passage. The heifer's back was illustrated by a dying sun, a wake of powdery flourishes faded like smoke in a stunning white light – the low moon's ripe fullness invoked pure allure – blooming, bursting.

"Best round 'em up now." Violet eyes caught Susan's, Davie was beside her. She must have been too rapt in the setting to hear his approach. He smiled. "You seen Rikki?"

"Rikki?" said Susan, as if the name were new to her ears. Swaying her trance-like essence and sorcery through shadowy

24

scenery, the secretive sphere's influence lacked time, movement. Boabs gleamed. Smooth bark shone. Susan spoke softly. "He galloped out too. Must have gone the wrong way, I guess."

"We'll jus' round 'em up together then."

Side by side they rode that night, horses stepping as one. It was as though they were aroused by some force in black bushes, enticed by mysteriously elusive moonlight, and drifted on guiding breezes. All around was motionless.

"Like a film set this. You 'n' me," said Davie, the silver on his face, "know what I mean?" She just felt the story unfolding. "Romantic 'ere, ridin' in moonlight." It touched Susan's cheek. "We could just gallop away, me 'n' you." And he could see her so clearly. "Like a film set this. Just you an' me." Precious time, stop ticking. "Ever been taken off a galloping horse?" There was no need to look to Susan. She had no thoughts; no need to dream. "I'll put my arm round you when we're galloping, done it plenty times. You'd be right."

Nothing would take that memory away. Davie spoke slowly while the cattle herded together naturally in the bewitching darkness of the pale moon's lightness. "I'll do that one day, take you off a galloping horse, you'll be right. You'll see."

There was security in the stockman's tones, the vulnerable voice she believed. The horses walked gracefully. They rode in silence as the land breathed out, the moon drew them in.

Susan didn't wait for Davie's call the next morning; she was up, showered, dressed and in for breakfast before dawn. Davie laid bread, milk, jam, tea on the black table, then set off across the track, melting into opaque blueness. Having eaten all she wanted, Susan went outside. Daylight washed the sky, from its depths shone a brilliant white star. Wrapped in her anorak Susan felt cold, her cheeks cut by the sharp sun-up air.

A distant engine spluttered and started, strained, grew closer;

the flat-faced buggy appeared. Davie drove, Pete and Rikki sat quiet in the back. Susan settled beside Davie. He put his foot down and they sped out in the direction of the water tower. Their destination, the stable block, was well within walking distance so Susan wondered why they had to drive.

Parked beside the shed at the far end of the block was a cattle truck, a sleeping driver at the wheel. The Canadian manager strolled over as Davie pulled up, and made a joke about working with the girl. His jest received a wintry lack of response.

The cattle truck had two decks, chaotically crammed with sturdy metal posts and spiked wire rolls. Susan was strong and willing; she worked in line with Pete and Rikki, forming a con-veyor belt lumbering to and from the nearby shed with heavy goods that punctured skin. Each roll of barbed wire was three foot in diameter, with a short wooden pole through the centre of a few of them. It was easier to carry these; others had to be hoisted any ungainly way they could. The Canadian manager crouched in the doorway of the truck, throwing barbed rolls out into dust, or skilfully negotiating the end of a pole to reaching out, expectant hands.

Davie stacked the goods in the shed. From the corner of an eye, he watched Susan's deft, feminine movements. It was a tight squeeze in the doorway to the shed. Blocking Susan, Davie guiltily looked down. He was on edge, pursing his lips after each sentence.

"You don't 'ave to do this," he said with a mixture of concern and resentment. "You can do the cooking if you want."

Susan shook her head. "I'm happy as I am."

"'Ere, let me 'elp you." Davie hunched his shoulders. "'Ard work out 'ere, eh? You might be 'appier workin' in the kitchen." Susan hadn't come all this way to work in a kitchen, she didn't want to cook, especially now that Davie had given her a horse.

When she tired, with gentle force Davie urged Susan to rest and sit with him on the great, curved chrome front bumper of the truck.

Sunlight saturated the heat and later they all staggered, chins up, backs bent, hands dented from spiked wire. Dripping in sweat they finished the job. It was now clear to Susan why Davie had driven them there: after all that lifting and carrying, walking back to the bunk-house in the midday sun would have been too much. The return drive passed in grateful silence.

During lunch the Canadian told Susan that Bill Roberts wanted to have a word with her. After the meal she went to his study, knocked and entered.

In an airless, penitentiary box of an office, behind a white, severely gleaming expanse of desk, sat Bill Roberts, his tartan shirt starched, cuffs tucked double, khaki shorts encasing white-socked legs, well calved, bearing round red knees. A pen worked in his right hand, his left hand supported his head and the telephone receiver – an extension of his arm, which was propped on the desk. He nodded for Susan to be seated on the chair opposite.

"Okay, okay, I've got that," swelled Bill in a display of efficiency as he filled in columns of figures in a hard-backed A4 book. "I'll be in town Wednesday, Thursday, I'll have to go to Elders anyhow."

Replacing the receiver, the station manager eased back, raising his eyebrows expectantly; his covert smirk a disguise to conceal the content of his mind.

"Right, Susan, you've come to see me, I like that an' I'll let you into a little secret." Bill's eyebrows rose higher, then relaxed, he ruched in each shirt-sleeve. "I didn't want you 'ere, but when your friend Paddy rang I couldn't think of an excuse not to take you on. So, 'ere you are. How d'ya like High Rocky?"

"I like it, I like it a lot," she replied.

Bill felt inferior hearing English tones. Hatred began to rise. "If yous wanna stay you must prepare yourself for the consequences because I ain't takin' any cunts who don't know nothin'." Susan squirmed back into the chair. She found his words objectionable, but while Bill mawed on, realised that fortitude would be construed as a threat. Her sight wandered down to the account book on the desk, and in her mind's eye the columns of figures seemed to represent the straight lines of education that ruled her life. She looked at the computer, the calculator, the fax; lifeless possessions stared back.

Susan gathered that Bill Roberts treated his workforce abysmally, without a trace of remorse. He leant forward. "You die 'ere, that's your problem. I'm gonna put you in yer place. I don't think you're suited to station life, you're inexperienced round cattle. *You* should be paying *me* to work 'ere." Forearms squarely in front of him, Bill shunted, resettled and resumed his lecture. Susan's thoughts floated to Davie, to the piebald in the corral that needed water. "You'll put your work for me before all yer needs, think of me, treat me as your god. You want this place to be your world?"

Still looking down, Susan nodded, wishing he would let her get back to work. "Yes, sir."

"So if this place is your world what am I?" Bill exuded hatred. Susan didn't know what to say. "*God*!" the manager clamoured, banging the desk. "I am your god! I'm takin' you on a trial basis, then we'll see, we'll see how you get on in the yard. But I don't want you 'ere, don't forget that I'll be doin' you a favour by lettin' you stay each day."

Susan acknowledged this subserviently.

"Don't thank me," came a curt scowl, "I don't want you 'ere."

Getting up to go, she wondered whether to ask Bill Roberts if he would like to be referred to as God from now on, then thought better of it.

On the third morning Susan walked to the kitchen block in darkness. Davie prepared the breakfasts; he had already eaten his. Pete, Rikki and the girl ate at the table in silence.

28

Davie directed his words at Susan. "Today we gonna muster a mob o' cattle 'n' drive 'em into the yard. You workin' today?"

"Yes, sure."

"You sure? Don't 'ave to, y'know."

Susan felt quite sure.

"I'll have to teach you how to handle the horse in cattle an' drove right."

Davie gave Susan a proper stock horse, saying it was her gun horse, the best horse for her to ride when there was a lot of work to do. The bright-eyed mare was fifteen hands high, velvety brown with a black mane and tail and a pure white diamond on her forehead. Susan immediately fell in love with the horse and felt silly because no one else seemed attached to theirs.

Horses were part of Davie's life; he treated them with kindness, they responded accordingly. He knew better than to pamper them the way Susan did. He told her his eldest brother had taught him how to spay bulls, cut cows, lasso and rope clean-skin cattle to bring them from the scrub to the yard for branding. Poddy dodging, they called it, he never thought of it as stealing. In the wet he cut wattle for pegs to make hobbles, and made rope out of rawhide. They got no pay, just clothes, tucker, a bluey, sticks of tobacco. Davie told Susan how, in the old days, the ringers had three horses each. Susan thought, How grand.

Swiftly they cantered through a copse, brushing bush, after cows who, when startled, broke cover and fled under drooping branches, skimming fallen trunks. When horned bulls bolted for open spaces, Pete and Rikki galloped after the red trail-blazers, tearing over a wind-swept plain. Pete excelled to the hilt, racing neck-and-neck with a well-ribbed beast, yanked the bull's tail, jerking the runaway beast off balance; impulsively Pete flung himself from the roan, crashing the bull to the ground in plumes of dust. Rikki, upon the bull's rump, tugged the tail taut between the hind legs to keep the fallen beast down. Pete thrashed the spirit from the heated animal so it wouldn't take to flight again.

29

They chased cattle cavorting into dust, rounded them into a herd. That day they mustered one hundred wild cattle and drove them into the yard. The men argued as they pedantically head-counted in the dusty flamingo-glow of dusk.

Davie praised Susan's efforts at mustering; she was dependent on him in his world of which she knew so little and from this dependency a firm bond grew. They worked together as a team; although at first she slowed the others down, each dawn her strength increased. Conversation was limited. Pete and Rikki spoke in low hushed tones, rarely to Susan; tentative Davie only when necessary. Her ears were soothed by their sensuous voices, their mutual rapport. She called them "my mob" because that was what they would say. The title "mob" was used consistently.

The girl learned their patois, she went everywhere with Davie and his black posse: he said that she belonged, she felt an affinity and an inner sense of belonging. Her sentiment was augmented by a strange dream in which she drifted through time itself, trawling continents with a net cast wide, flew back far, homing in on ancient bloodlines, divining a fraternity of kindred spirit – a fanciful vision, mythical perhaps, more valuable and meaningful to the soul than scientific proof, as evocative and rhetorical as the native black swan.

Being the only woman on the camp had its difficulties. Days stretched out like a full concertina, nights ran by close and condensed, but Susan soon settled into the work. She rode well with the mare, who was slender and gentle, nervous at the start of the day, perfectly trained to muster. Her trot was keen, her canter smooth as flying. The mare galloped after saucy cows, veering them in, shouldering them round, chasing them back to the herd.

After a month of working on horseback in the rugged beauty of the Kimberley, Susan was glowing through and through. It was exhilarating to gallop through long golden grasses after cattle engulfed in dust when wallabies, sand goanna, desert lizards scattered, the sun sinking red, full moon rising high.

Susan thought it must be Wednesday. They hadn't had any time off since she arrived, each day felt much like the last. They were up at 3 a.m. tuberculosis testing, then she drove a clapped-out Toyota truck across sun-baked scrub after Davie, Rikki and Pete, who were driving three hundred head of cattle. Her jeans were gritty with dirt from the outback and she could see from the state of the truck it would be one of those dusty jobs. Her task was to pick up the tiny calves that dropped from exhaustion in the heat. She would rather have been on horseback but because she was "the girl", she got the odd jobs when they occurred. Derby had been cooling down a bit when Susan left, here it was humid, very hot.

Her mob were able horsemen; Susan watched as they drove. Clouds of dust surrounded them as they sauntered through the herd; elegant horses cantered and galloped so freely, effortlessly, under stockmen scolding cattle. A good horse and rider worked as one, moved as one; in unison their bodies swerved, this way and that. Cattle would turn threateningly at a man on the ground, yet they respected the horses and rarely charged. Susan always laughed when they were driving cattle and one of the men had to chase a frisky calf that suddenly got a mind of its own, skitting from the herd. Chasing a rogue bull or cow on horseback looked magnificently macho, but week-old calves were terribly difficult to round up because they were so comically scant, making a mockery of those fine men.

They had a break for a couple of hours; it was too hot to work. The cattle were languorous, would drop if pushed on. They were driving the cattle in from their land. The best steers would be sent to the meat works, and they had a long way to go. Distances in cattle country weren't measured in miles or kilometres, the men just said, "We gotta pass four bores; four windmills." Susan didn't know how far that was. Maybe five or six hours. And time was not measured by a watch, the men just went by how they felt. They rose with the morning star, when thirsty boiled the billy, when hungry had a feed and when too tired they turned in.

They were on the move again. It was cooler then. Sundown. Rikki found a patch of baby watermelon in the bush. Pink ones. And they ate them whole as they moved cattle on. Davie said he ate the pips and he told Susan she should too, then he said he was a bird. A white cockatoo. And a flock of white cockatoos rose silently, silver from a tree, and Susan laughed, Davie laughed, then they all laughed together.

Imagine the relief as the heat of the day died, everything earthly turned to gold and the sky was blue-grey, heavy with rain they would not see fall. It was dusty, Susan was filthy, sticky with watermelon juice, while her head resounded with the sounds of cattle, the crack of the head stockman's whip. All good things seemed to shatter and break into so many pieces. She could not begin to reconstruct time, places. Just the memory of feeling remained. Feeling placid. Passive. No want for anything. She understood how fragile life is; knowing this was good – a cascade, a waterfall of happiness descended. Timelessness seeped through her soul.

Dust rose over the cattle like mist in a valley. Two men with red shirts. One red cap, one blue cap. Two black horses dancing, weaving round the tail end of the drove where calves scampered with big deer-like eyes and turned-up noses, vanishing into golden spinifex grasses and a hazy sunset.

They had to finish droving in the dark and only reached the first bore. Pete warned Susan of spirits: "Don't get too far behind or they'll get you." The paddock gate was narrow, they must have lost around twenty head in the bottle-neck, pushing them through the dust and the dark.

There was a restlessness in the air. Six drunken lads, aged between sixteen and twenty, returned from a camp in the northern part of High Rocky. They were all to stay in the bunk-house where Davie and Susan slept. Dolour descended with their arrival.

The day's labour had been tiresome, the heat sweltering. Davie let them knock off early. By dusk it hadn't cooled down when he set on the length of black table four white enamel plates with their supper of beef, tinned carrots, peas and white sliced bread.

Rikki and Pete hovered at the table edge. Davie sat anxious. He spoke with integrity.

"You gotta eat, make you strong like me. Pete, Susan, Rikki, come 'n' 'ave a feed." They sank remorsefully on chairs. Davie was more despondent, more vexed than usual. The position of head stockman had been given to a white ringer because Bill Roberts didn't think it fitting for Davie to run the camp now that the white workers had returned.

An illicit silence hung in heavy familiar folds. Davie was as dignified as one can be with an undignified predicament. Pete and Rikki, sleepy after a feed of beef stew, cans in hands, eyes down. Uncommunicative. It was early for the men to be drinking.

Sadness welled inside Susan. She couldn't say how sorry she was – couldn't express pity. Pity, she felt, was poor charity. Hedging around the table with the idea of inspecting the store for any intriguing curiosities, she excused herself from the melancholy party.

The store, built of wooden slats, stood raised off the ground for coolness in summer and dryness in the wet. As Susan mounted the eroding wooden steps Carl called.

"Hey lady. You need anythin'?" He was parked against his light blue Cadillac, in front of his tumbledown bungalow, across the track from the shed; ten gallon hat tipped to shield his forehead, denim legs crossed; a classic ageing drover. "I'll get the keys if you need anythin'. 'Ave to get the keys from the station house, see, Shelley runs the store."

Susan said she didn't need anything, she was just having a look around.

"How's you doin' anyways?"

"Okay I think," she said, approaching demurely. "I mean I liked it here. I've hardly seen Bill. Guess I was being nosey."

"Well, I'm jus' fillin' in time too. Gunna have a look 'round my place? I'm headin' for Queensland at daybreak. You can stay at my place when I'm gawn." She asked Carl whether he had found "The Moon In The Kimberley", he said he hadn't, he'd look for it later, before he left. "You gotta git t' hear it y'know," he replied, "you'll really like it, that's for sure." Watching him running his fingers devotedly over the smooth, hot, polished bonnet, Susan could picture Carl caressing a faithful old nag at a long day's end. He stepped around the front of the car, unable to resist giving it a fond stroke and conclusive pat.

From the outside Carl's bungalow was no more than a dilapidated shack, deceptively small. The traditional front porch protruded from a corrugated iron roof. Despite the seasonal heat and dryness, it exuded a damp, fusty smell. There seemed to be little compensation in this harsh country.

A dingy hallway divided the interior, and Carl's decaying squalor. The first two rooms accommodated four absent-mindedly placed iron beds, supporting sagging mattresses, one had stained sheets, stripped back, flowing into a pool on the floor. The toilet and shower, where paint peeled, stank. Tiny bars of sloppily scattered orange soap stuck to the floor. Susan felt dirty and dejected just being there. The kitchen was a slum. A light bulb dangled from a cracked ceiling, the hue of blotchy mustard blemished with an irregular network of tea-coloured stains. The once white electric cooker was thickly greased in festering globules of fat, food and dust. In one corner a slovenly stack of soiled

34

plates was propped against the cooker on a scarred linoleum floor, grimly besmeared with warty growths. In fact, the whole interior, and its contents, Carl included, was caked in a decrepit film of grey, anile dust, reeking of dreary solitude, drunkenly prepared meals and mouldy, rancid fat.

The old man was clearly proud of his habitat, it had served as home, a retreat from his domineering son. "Yous wanna stay 'ere?"

"Mmm. Maybe. Thanks," was all Susan could think of to say, with a sated smile for Carl's eagerness.

"Come to Queensland if ya like, I've been waiting for ya."

Susan felt a pang of compassion for the redundant drover with his unpopular son and would have liked to have said yes, to see the gratitude, the joy in those steady blue eyes filled with futile hopes. She could feel his appreciation at having a companion for a while and felt sure he deserved more, there, obsolete, nearing the end of a lonesome road; in this genre he would inevitably pass away.

"I like it here, Carl. I like High Rocky, and Davie, you know. I don't feel like moving yet," explained Susan. She then agreed to share the evening with him.

Carl grabbed a stash of beer from the fridge and he and Susan sat in the Cadillac with the windows wound down for what seemed like hours, listening to dated tapes, watching the light fade and seeking "The Moon In The Kimberley". Carl introduced her to the patriotic songs of Slim Dusty, and a full moon rose in the starlit sky.

The time, Susan decided, had come to leave. Carl, who was by then revelling in the past – how uncompromising his woman had been – and downing Emu with intemperance, had other ideas.

"Stay 'ere. Stay the night wiv me," exclaimed the drover with abandon, limply swinging his arm from the car window.

Jeez, thought Susan, this man is old enough to be my father, no, grandfather. She would have liked to have given him a hug, bless him, to show there were no hard feelings, but realised it would be safer to save any affection for a morning farewell. She quickly said goodnight, opened the Cadillac's door and slipped out into the night.

Heading for the bunk-house, Susan thought of Davie's demoralised stance. The moon shone softly on High Rocky's hilltops, icing peaks of distant mountains, bathing the station in a splendid snowy light. A semicircle of ringers barred the entrance to the bunk-house. Davie reminisced to them, clinging to the old times; the young men listened, bringing in the new. They were seated on chairs planted steadfast in dust, bodies attentively curled forward, elbows on knees, a can in hand, a stash of cans at their feet. To delay their encounter, Susan altered direction, walking right, past empty swags on the plinth to enter the brightly lit kitchen.

Pete and Rikki sat side by side at the expansive black table. At first they had not drunk much, a couple of Emu a night at the most. An endless supply was shelved, cool in the station house fridge, waiting to be deducted from meagre wages.

Pete greedily slurped at a can, Rikki murmured, rolling a cigarette in one hand. The noises niggled, but the blanket of silence still smothered.

Susan poured a cup of tea from a steaming kettle on the cooker, sat down opposite them and asked if Davie was all right.

Rikki struck a match. Cigarette lit, he began turning the tobacco tin over and over on the table top, tapping, like a dripping faucet. Pete gave a muffled reply.

"'Im outside. By 'em bunk-house, with 'em ringers."

Rikki dropped the tobacco tin, they all jumped, the blanket – never ruffled. He picked up the tin, with a feckless grunt, resumed tapping.

The men downed Emu, Susan blew on hot tea. All stared at the egg-stained table.

"What are we doing tomorrow?" asked Susan.

"Stackin' straw for 'em horses," came Rikki's answer.

Eventually Pete rose to fetch more cans from the top compartment of the fridge. He handed one to Rikki.

"Ay, you wanna drink?"

Susan said okay.

The beer was tepid, it didn't mix too well in a stomach full of hot tea. "Thanks," she said. "I'll finish this in my room." Pete and Rikki looked nonplussed and bade her goodnight.

Knowing things would be different at High Rocky, Susan peered across the dark track. The temperature had finally dropped; the cattleman, the moonlit ringers, seemed less of a daunting obstacle. They didn't notice the girl until she was virtually in their midst. Then their eyes uplifted and the group stirred: there was a forceful unity in their strength and determination, solidarity in their resistance. There had been too many newcomers to this country.

Davie's eyes stung as he shifted territory. "Say 'ello to the boys." Shuffling his body forward, he gestured to the clean-shaven, fair-haired white youth opposite, and used the tone he had when he and Susan had first met, the tone Davie used to calm a frightened animal.

"This is Greg Palmer. 'E's 'ead stockman, 'e is. You gotta work fer 'im now, Greg. 'E's 'ead stockman round 'ere now, see."

Greg stood too hastily, steadying himself on the back of the chair with one hand. "Pleased to meet you." A resolute voice, his callow face clenched. The face went blank again, not a muscle moved. It seemed an unnaturally formal debut for such a queer setting. Susan hated the manager for replacing Davie with the stranger.

Greg sat down. "This is Ray," he said courteously, looking to his left. Ray and Susan nodded at each other, exchanging uncomfortable glances. Greg worked his way around the circle, introducing each in turn. Some of the beery bravado drained out of those young men and with it, some of Susan's trepidation.

Davie bade the girl goodnight and continued to tell old drovers' tales.

In the bunk-house Susan lit a candle and, out of a headscarf, made a primitive curtain for the little square of window. They were only a bunch of boys, she reasoned, there was nothing to be afraid of. She rolled a cigarette and lay, watching smoke streaks waft. Hearing them trudge in one by one, she snuffed out the candle.

There was darkness. Silence. A rustle. Davie's hesitant knock, his strained half whisper at the door.

"Can I come in?"

"Who is it?"

"Can I come in?"

"Yes, Davie, what do you want?"

Susan watched the handle dip. Closing the door behind him, Davie stopped. "Shhh," he hushed.

Sensing turbulence in his mind, she waited. The bulk of his frame trembled so violently it seemed to send out improvident ripples of moonshine.

Davie whispered urgently, notes of a quashing agony rang poignant through his words. "You all right?"

"Yes, Davie."

"Shhh. Shhh." He looked agitated in muted moonlight, fretful form exaggerated by cruel shadows. Susan felt surprisingly calm and hoped that it might help to quell this anguish if she spoke his name.

He winced and shivered. "Shhh." Then sank into silence.

"Davie, what do you want?"

There was a pause. He appeared to have lapsed to another plane and, on hearing her voice, returned to this world in a complete quandary, riddled with dismay, shaking his head.

Quietly he let himself out. She heard him struggle with his boots, collide with the door, tumble on the swag, turn over a couple of times, sigh.

THEY SPENT the next week drafting cattle in the yard. From her roost under the shade of an old eucalyptus, Susan had a clear view of the layout: at a glance, a nonsensical maze of pens with gates leading off one another, yet, as she observed, she quickly saw an intricate pattern to the procedure of drafting or yarding up.

In its entirety the yard was circular, a cattle race ran in a semicircle inside the boundary fence. Each herd was driven into the holding pen (an expanse of sand trimming the paddock behind the yard) and guided to a gate that opened on to the yard's chief, wedge-shaped compound, which could be sub-divided by swing gates into three sizable folds. The cattle could then gradually be cordoned off in smaller pens, or fed towards the cattle race.

The race, wide enough for one full-grown beast to pass, had four sub-divisions split by sturdy, sliding scaffolding gates, thus enabling control of the flow of cattle into smaller groups or, individually, to a tiny pen at the end. Each side of the tiny pen could be opened, and from here the final stage of drafting took place: individual cattle were routed to various enclosures where calves, bullocks, cows and stock for the meat works were cut out and kept separate.

Running up like a gang-plank from the front of the tiny pen to an elevated platform was a narrow ramp with wooden floorboards framed by a tall scaffolding structure. Road trains drew up alongside the platform for stock workers to load cattle destined for the meat works.

In the centre of the yard was a circular arena, easily accessible from any of the surrounding pens. This was the safest part of the yard. Whoever was in charge dictated orders and instructions from the arena, and the sliding gates to the cattle race were operated from there. A drinking trough was in an enclosure to the right of centre. To centre left, a little wooden shed with an iron roof stabled a black oil drum, branding equipment and neatly stacked paint tins. Sick calves were slippered inside, paint-dipped sticks leant against the open entrance.

A well-trodden track led from the yard through the holding pen to a windmill screened by crooked trees, scrawny bushes and the wattle that tenuously grew from stony red earth. This track continued past an elongated water trough alongside a fence which could be hoisted up on poles for cattle to pass below. At the end of the track sat a fat boab under whose leafy hood were three black oil drums. It was in the shade of the boab that Susan and Davie had smoko and lunch. They let the horses loose in a paddock as the sun set, and stocked the yard full so the cattle would be settled before the next day's work.

The first time Susan was charged by a wild steer she was in the shade of the eucalyptus outside the yard. Nostrils a-quiver, brown bulk snorting, horned head poised; the most intimidating were his bulbous eyes. A powerful hoof pawed red dust then thunder rushed towards her. The instant the bullock charged Susan fell back flat in a flurry of dust.

As if on cue, Davie was faithful at her side.

"'E 'l right, won't 'urt you. Got the fence 'ere, see. You gotta be careful when you *in* the yard." He chuckled sympathetically, patting a scaffolding bar.

Surprised that she hadn't been trampled to death, Susan raised her head.

Davie laughed reassurance. "'E jus' a bit wild, but 'e won't hurt you through this fence."

Susan was too shocked to see the absurdity of her reaction, her bones were stiff and bruised from riding, standing up seemed insufferable.

Davie stooped to pick up a hefty stick in one hand, the other coaxed Susan forward, then yanked her to her feet; not sparing her time to dust off, he mounted the scaffolding, and dropped from the bars into the congestion of cattle in the red dirt corral.

"Come on, this mob's right. No good if you're 'fraid of 'em, they can sense fear. Always watch out though."

Cautiously Susan clambered over railings into the compound. Davie's arms swished air like the blades of a windmill, the signal alarmed the advanced steer.

"Ya! Ya! Ya!" heralded Davie. The distressed beast cowered, bowing innocently, was swallowed in the herd's camouflage of inquisitive brown and white faces that withdrew in a slow, round-about way.

"You gotta watch out for these mongrels, sometimes there's a mad one. Mad cows is worser than a mad bull sometimes, but most of them're okay." Davie hesitated, frowning, moody-blue eyes transparently tentative, sweat trickling down the stubble of his cheeks. Susan diffidently grabbed at a strip of torn tartan shirt on Davie's back.

Brandishing his staff at adventurous cattle, Davie, proud as any care-abandoned matador, marched alongside the corral fence. Susan slunk in his footsteps with a pounding heart, clinging to frayed material in the pitiable terror of being impaled on a steer's horn and tossed up in the air like a sandbag on a bayonet.

"Stay wiv me, I got a big stick 'ere, see," cajoled Davie over his shoulder.

Mid-way the stockman stopped. His hands waved freely at curious cattle, he shooed, warning them. "Wrraa, wrraa. Gitcha!" As though a galvanic power pulsed through them, the herd shrank back. "Right now, I'll watch out for you. Jus' keep close to the sides, then if one goes for you, you can 'op over like dis, see." The shirt was wrenched from Susan's grip as Davie heaved himself high into the air, his legs swinging over the top rail in an acrobatic leap.

"Yah, yah," she grinned in gleeful doubt.

Davie squinted through rusty rails, smiling wryly. "You'd do it if you 'ad to." He hopped back over. Susan reached for the shirt, cunningly he swanned aside to evade her hand as he hitched up his jeans, wobbled on his boots, and wiped the sweat away. "Jus' walk through, see," said Davie in a matter of fact tone.

When they had completed the length of the corral the stockman used a shirt-sleeve to mop the sweat from his brow. "Where's me stick?" He clowned about, spinning circles, dragging his feet in a rising cloak of rosy dust. He released a stout laugh. "No worries. Right, you lead, I follow."

Davie's hands waved the girl on as though she were a cheeky fly. Banking on Davie being behind, she turned to rework their tracks: her eyes fixed on the eucalyptus tree by the loading landing, she didn't dare look back or at the cattle until she reached assurance – the scaffolding on the far side of the corral. Filled with trust she mounted the rails, turned precariously and thankfully seated the highest pole.

Davie had given Susan the slip, had climbed over the scaffolding at the far end of the corral where he dawdled with Greg. Susan knew Davie had watched her from the corner of his eye, she could tell from the stockman's ostentatious gait that he was pleased with the success of his trick, and her first lesson in the yard.

The yard was like a rehearsing circus: full of unknown dramas, dangers, new acts to learn. It was also the dustiest place Susan had ever been. By dusk a drowsy cloud reddened and lurked; creeping into ears, it penetrated noses, throats, clogged the pores, seeping through sinuses to fog the brain.

They watered cattle tormented by the sun's sabotage, in the yard, or beyond at the trough near the paddock, in either case the ground rapidly became a puckered muddy mire. Slurping, sloshing, supple tails swishing, long tongues slipping and sliding in and out of nostrils, lethargic eyelashes lazily dozed, opened and closed. All were eager for their turn at the trough as the heat waned and flies surrendered to the evening.

In the temporary light of sundown they undid horses' girths at the ring, removing saddles and blankets moulded to steaming backs. Susan and Rikki rode bare-back to the trough to sloosh sweat-encrusted hides while the horses drank luxuriously.

Slinky as seals, naked but for bridles, the pack were led out to turf.

"Don't believe it when people say nature is caring – when we're gone they kick the shit outa each other, this mob," Rikki said to Susan as she hung harness on the fence.

"We gotta give 'em a feed yet," reminded Davie. Then he and Susan would drive all the way back to the station stable-block to load the buggy with hay.

"I'm pretty crook from dis dust, y'know. 'Ad enough o' dis mongrel car 'n' all," choked Davie, pulling up on concrete for them to tug prickly bale upon bale from the stack, hauling them into the truck, hitching a trailer to the tow bar and filling that too. Each bale felt heavier than the last. They struggled inordinately, enduring the strain with rope-cut hands; their bodies, weightless shells emancipated when they paused for smoko.

Smoke danced and ducked, wraiths waving in dusk while the glow of the sky turned from blue-mauve to orange-white and fluorescent light pink. The sulphurous scent of wood smoke, sourly musky and spicy from somewhere embalmed, and Susan's only concern was that her jeans needed washing.

Davie switched the headlights on, a flock of jeering grey-backed galah spiralled, crimson undersides turning in the

43

half-light as the ugly buggy screamed back to the yard through a dust-hovering sunset.

The smell of drafting prevailed, it hugged the fluted track and hampered their breathing. Susan wondered whether they'd ever breathe freely again.

Davie's elbow nuzzled her ribs. "'Ere!" shouted the stockman against the engine noise, mindfully drawing a red and white handkerchief from his pocket, aggressively shoving it between her knees. "Take dis, tie 'im round yer face. 'Elps stop the dust from getting up yer nose. Make you crook, dis dust. Can't wait to be away from this place," he confided.

"Me too," murmured Susan, not knowing whether he meant the yard, or High Rocky, too tired to care.

The sky was pitch black by the time they returned. It was cold too. Headlights poorly lit a row of ringers' faces at the loading platform, nesting like indistinct birds resting on a fence. Crickets chirped, cattle lowed, beds beckoned, yet there was much more to do that night.

First they launched bales into the horses' paddock. Those demons in darkness bared their teeth, flattened their ears back and snapped. Pete hoisted bales over the yard fence to cattle, whilst Susan, masked with Davie's handkerchief, armed with a penknife, skirted the inside of the enclosures, sawing the twine that held bales firm until *twang*, they yawned open and could be shaken into slices.

Working hurriedly, fearful of munching, marauding cattle, she scattered the hay around the fence side, and wound retrieved twine round her hands. One heifer lunged forward as Susan shook a bale loose. "Fuck off, ya mongrel," she wailed, reassured by the vernacular tones, skimming the rails in swift retreat.

Black shapes loomed. The sky looked thick, air suffocated, crickets crooned, beasts' belches reverberated. Voices were face-less in darkness. Davie spoke.

"You 'ear anythin'?"

"Who?"

"Sshh. There's a truck comin'. Me'be ten miles away."

They sat on the fence in the pitch dark, cold poles biting bottoms, shadows crept, cud-chewing cattle snoozed. Susan didn't know if she fell asleep, sore on the rail, biding time. Davie's voice brought back reality.

"Can 'ear it now. Can you 'ear it? I can 'ear it definite. Mus' be close now. You'll 'ear it if yer put yer ear t'the ground. You cold?"

"Yeah."

"Fuck dis. Truck's comin' now." And sure enough a deep purr vibrated, aberrant in black emptiness. "Watch out for dem snakes."

"Where?"

"I don't know," he mumbled designlessly, jumping from the rail. "Fuckin' everywhere."

A rumble in the mountains grew into a blinding main beam, and big rolling wheels ensued by a sluggish stream of glaring red tail-lights. The road train grumbled to a standstill. It was when the moon disappeared behind clouds, and dust and dirt rose from the feet of the cattle, that Susan was most afraid.

With electronic prodders they loaded bullocks in the dark to yells of "Ya! Ya! Gitcha!", "Fuckin' ugly cow!", "Git up there, mongrels!", "Huh. Huh. Git up there!", "Git up!" Couldn't see much though. Couldn't see anything really; tramping under heaven's murky diamonds, Susan's fear of cattle had fled by the early hours. Somebody hollered, "This the last one?"

"Yeah, 'e's last."

It was a cold drive back to the station. They had no tucker and were too tired to feel remotely refreshed by a tepid shower.

Susan was too tired even to wash her filthy jeans; not scared that snakes might be under the bed any more. She unrolled her swag and dropped. Relief. There was a knock at the door; a pause. The creaking handle dipped, a hand poked round, releasing a bundle.

"'Ere. You can 'ave dees. You done good, y'know. Goo'night."

"Thanks, Davie. Goodnight." Susan rose to investigate, felt the crumpled heap, in darkness shook two items of clothing free. A pair of Davie's baggy, threadbare corduroys and a short-sleeved cotton shirt. They smelt fresh. He must have read her mind.

Leaving the clothes strewn on the floor, she fell back on her swag. The bed groaned, inane warmth spread.

Davie was always first to be ready. Susan assisted with chores in the kitchen, then they ambled to the lofty wooden shed across from the track where Bill's black stallion grazed. Davie would mutter as he checked vehicles, mended a puncture, filled up with fuel. Streaked by slits of sunlight sneaking through splintered chinks in the roof, he'd tinker with tools, gather grummets of rope, an odd assortment of musty, broken saddles, twisted bridles, blankets, rusty stirrup irons and other beneficials for the day's labour. Then Davie's mob, packed in anoraks and that rackety open-top buggy, roared out to the cattle yard to the commotion of scores of screeching galah under glorious golden skies.

Straggly haired Rikki and Pete, mere silhouettes etched by the sun, sprang from the back to open the main gate where the buggy swung round in a whirl of dust, veering left, passing far expanses of grassland to head for the indigo line of mountains.

The windscreen was soon coated in dirt and rattled so much that Davie might stop to flip it back on its hinges, clipping it to the bonnet. Susan relished that morning drive: thin air fresh with intoxicating fragrance, their eyes streaming from the rush of cold as they bobbed and bounced, the track rough and serrated throwing them up and down. Snuggled shoulder to shoulder with Davie, her senses impassioned, Susan would inhale anticipation while her stomach sloshed with sugary tea and toast. Feeling such rapture she drifted asleep, waking with a jolt as Davie pulled up at the yard fence.

The horses' coats shone in the sun-up light, their eyes were bright as buttons when one by one the stockmen singled them into an empty pen to be cornered and caught by each one's rider. Bill Roberts arrived later, fettered by the previous evening's drinking session.

He stood clean and immaculate by the shed in the centre of the cattle yard, correctly adorned in Akubra, white shirt, khaki shorts, long white socks, brown boots. At his side, a miniature manager, like father, indolently digesting a breakfast of bacon and eggs. Under unassuming sunlight, this virulent pair in matching regimentals looked strangely out of place.

It was the hottest day yet. The stock workers ambled into the yard, they were to start TB testing. Some cattle would be daubed with a paint-dipped stick that left a messy white splodge on their hides. Susan never fully understood that procedure though, simple as it may have been.

Davie, in a blue shirt and moleskins, slumped a shoulder against a rail at the back of the second fold; absorbing the play of the sun, his blue cap peak pointed to red ground.

Susan chose to work the gate at the first fold. She stepped on the lowest rung, faced out to pasture, draped her arms over the top pole and awaited imminent orders.

Greg entered the arena. His face was always thin-lipped, the worn leather chaps polished at the loins, a downy speckled feather decked his hat.

Susan looked round at the manager. Hatred for his mercenaries had begun to rise. Bill Roberts' voice boomed.

"Git over to the race. *You* can work the gates today." Bill booted the butt of a ringer. The unprepared youth was propelled into the air with one powerful kick, thrust across the yard. "Git over there!" screamed Bill through gritted teeth. The ringer nose-dived, landing face down in dirt. Bill was upon the victim before he had time to stand. The dialogue remained one way, each word punctuated with a kick. Bill's sadistic nature overwhelmed him in its complicated manner. He swore horribly, striking the ringer's stomach as he writhed and coiled. Cursing again, Bill kicked the spine. The ringer curled, gulping. Words bit as the thud of boots hit.

Bill felt mean with low esteem. Teeth still gritted, he eased off the body, turning to address a bemused audience.

"All right! When I speak you should all jump. *Jump!* Hear me? Susan, fuckin'-work-the-gates."

"Yes, sir." Jogging to the race as she spoke. Susan didn't know how to work the gates yet. Bill knew it was a bad choice.

"Okay. Why isn't anyone in that first pen?" No answers.

"*Why isn't anyone in the first pen?*" blared Bill. Davie trundled to the pen.

"*Why* isn't anyone in that next pen?"

Pete regarded the manager with quiet, aloof cynicism. His frail black figure reposed on the rails of the second fold, his Akubra rim's shadow obscuring his features; by lifting his head he revealed himself, as if to coolly say, "Yeah, I bin 'ere all th' time."

"Okay. Why isn't there anyone at this gate?" The body on the ground in front of Bill twitched. "Boy," bawled Bill at his son. "Fuckin' git in that pen." Roaring, Bill lashed out at the bewildered child with his boot.

The ringer afoot dragged himself upright, clutching his stomach, sloped towards the gate. He was new. He took off the next day. Bill's son ran across the yard. Greg sprinted ahead, outstripping the child and the ringer.

Bill nodded approbation. "Okay. I've got work to do in my office. Greg, I'm leaving you in charge."

What Greg Palmer took from Bill's grossly unmitigated exhibitions he gave out on the animals. His first victim was the old Brahmin bull.

The Brahmin bull was obstinate. It had taken four days in the yard to test his herd, each day the bull refused to walk past the gates of the first enclosure. Someone would crack Davie's whip over the bull's back, shouting to urge him on.

The Brahmin's response was unrelated. Flicking the willowy quiff of his tail, perhaps he'd dip his majestic head with its watery nose and glassy eyes. He might take a few paces back so the pendulums of skin hanging like leaden sacks about his neck modestly swung, and the distinguished mound on top of his shoulders flopped to one side before he firmly resumed his posture. Not that it mattered whether he walked through the race or not, he'd be turned out to pasture after testing was done. Greg had observed this routine procedure.

The bull's massive body stood motionless as he took his regal morning doze.

"Susan!" barked Greg. She jumped from a rung, hitching up an abundance of Davie's corduroys, gathered in bulky wads by her belt. "You workin' that first gate?"

"Yup."

"Git that Brahmin through then." Susan discreetly grinned to Davie. No one had managed to move that old bull. Being afraid of him, she was last person there suitable to do the job. Eyes wide, she strutted nonchalantly alongside the rails, towards the start of the holding enclosure.

Davie, head hurriedly shaking, "Nah, you're right," was up, over the poles and positioned to drive the Brahmin towards the race before Susan reached her destination.

Mild words from Davie. "Hey boy, move on." The bull snorted as though he knew he had pushed his luck.

Stock whip in hand, Greg was immediately upon them. Davie caught Susan's eye. His smirk withered, already defeated, he made way for Greg.

Leaning from behind the safety of the rails, Greg licked air with the whip. "Move, cunt." Thwack. He brought the whip down on the beast's bony back. Greg cursed again. Whack.

Swaying a little, the bull slowly, extremely reluctantly took two paces forward. Then halted. Greg was enraged. He thrashed the beast's back, motions, a series of tense, aggressive jerks. Thwack. He cursed and whacked.

Pete, Rikki and Ray left their posts to assemble along the rails. Greg sliced the back imperatively. The bull's head lowered, he took two short steps back. "*Mo*-ove forw-*ard*!" demanded Greg. The bull stood still. His soft eyes dreamily gazed, the wet black nose shone, there was a tremor on the grey flank from an itch on his sagging coat.

Greg was furious. He ducked between the scaffolding railings and stomped right up behind the bull, who simply sighed wearily, lowering his head further. "Ya! Ya! Yaa!" cursed Greg, kicking squalls of dirt at the beast's rear. To everyone's relief the beast strolled into the empty enclosure ahead, hump lolling, and stopped by the railings. "Ya! Ya! Yaa!" The animal regarded Greg's efforts with renewed indifference. "Fuckin' *move*!" Greg mounted the railings, shinning up until his chest was level with the bull's spine, then, in a vicious gesture at the animal's arrogance, burrowed the whip handle into a flabby grey flank, growling, "Move, move. Move!" He stabbed between great ribs, curvaceous as a ship's upturned skeleton, prodding and snarling demonically.

Exasperated, Greg, hurling abuse, surmounted the top rail and reached himself across to sit right on the bull. The bull trembled; his thickset legs didn't budge. Greg faced backwards, his ropy torso whetted with perspiration, the veins on his forehead full-blown. The cowboy looked small and mean astride that mountainous back. Edging out, inch by inch, impending spurs winking at the sun, he stretched over curvaceous haunches, reaching so far forward that Davie thought he might topple off. Greg groped for the bull's tail. He raised the stiffly held tube and

50

prized it back in an arc. The bull snorted. In one hand Greg tightly gripped the tail, about three inches from the end. Clasping the wiry black tassel in the other, he clenched his jaw, ground his teeth and his green eyes flared with the glib prowess of red-necked cowboys amidst cheering crowds applauding a rodeo rigged for their success: gibing rodeo clowns with painted faces streaming while smarmy charlatans taunt frenzied, sand spraying bulls and black men shadow, hosing dust dead.

Greg swallowed, his jutting adam's apple bobbed, thick-ribbed forearms rippled and braced and, crack, he snapped the end of the bull's tail. The old bull sighed, but did not take a step forward. Greg cracked another bone. In oppressive heat the sick sound sent a wave of repulsion through the ringers. Greg proceeded to crack another bone in the tail, a little further up. Here the tail was thicker, the noise more definite. He continued to break the bull's tail all the way up until it hung limply. The discomfort resulting from that show lasted, one of the bull's defences was gone for life, he could no longer whip away the plagues of flies that destroyed his peace.

Greg dismounted the bull's back; clambering back on to the rails, he climbed from the scaffolding into the yard. Thwack! Thwack! Thwack! He brought the whip down. An assortment of Akubras hid disdainful expressions: all the ringers willed that bull to move.

Thwack! Greg screamed obscenities behind the bull. Thwack! Screaming. Thwack! Screaming. Stumpy legs loosened, heavily the grim old monarch stepped out, slowly walking the length of the enclosure. Greg marched behind, cruelly cracking the whip overhead. Into the race the bull walked, his tattered, badly fitting coat touched both sides of the scaffolding. That old bull never hurt anyone. He was a fine beast. With a look that said he had known all along what was required, the bull plodded into the final pen. Greg had overtaken him, climbed into the central arena,

51

and opened the gate into the bull's enclosure. The Brahmin slothfully entered, then halted. He knew he was all right there.

Davie's words blurted out. He was furious. "I can't work in a place like this."

"Go then," returned Greg. He was shackled in shame. Turning clumsily, he couldn't look at Davie. No one looked at anyone else. Davie glared at the ground; speechless, hurting with humiliation. He'd done a stint at High Rocky before. He strolled out to the watering trough.

At nightfall, dishevelled by supersedure, unhinged Davie vainly washed his disgraceful rage – the injury of injustice – with Emu. When he cooked the evening meal Susan stood close by, vacantly making helpful gestures.

In water warmed by the sun, they soaked their jeans in the sink. Something slipped along the window sill, near Davie's nose. He was too tired to look up. He was aware of them in moonlight when the python married their bodies on the plinth outside the bunk-house. Susan secured her sarong, strung the washing out, watching snakes slither and hiss. Then Davie held her to his clammy chest which was hairy and soft and yet so strong: the moon hid her face, but Susan saw her in his wistful eyes when they stood heart to heart in darkness; the snakes eloped in the paddock where Bill's black stallion grazed.

When the chained dog slept for the witching time, in the dimmed shadows of the corridor, the sombre stockman smoked, remembering Mistake Creek where he had been born. They had never flogged the women but Davie had seen his best friend stripped, whipped with a belt until he near pegged out. That was the night they shot his pup for barking. The police were the Aboriginal Protectors then. Many years ago they had brought his great grandfather in from the desert and handed him to the station manager, who had a permit to work him as a slave and keep him prisoner. He didn't know the date when his great grandfather took off in a group. The manager had gone out with a search party, and herded them back to the station. Grandmother was ordered to go build a fire, great grandfather was tied to a tree, shot in the knee, and burnt as an example, while the others watched at gunpoint.

As the nippy sky dawned a brilliant star, the sentinel left his cold post; he wanted to leave the past behind; but Davie remembered many broken men who were the backbone of the cattle industry. Monstrous flames and burning shrieking great grandfather were all about him when he drove the truck back to the yard.

That morning the docile bull succumbed and walked through the race ahead of his herd. He did not pause to stop and think. His hump lolloped, loose furls of his coat flapped, the mutilated tail jolted painfully as his judicious head agreed to mark each steady plod of his great cracked hooves.

F OR THE FOLLOWING two months the work load was incredible. It was rumoured that there might be a break of one day, and the routine of rising in darkness to a shower and breakfast continued.

One Tuesday a herd was mustered in by helicopter. Susan watched the cattle shining with health canter down the foothills, then Greg Palmer's ringers drove the beasts to the cattle yard.

After the muster and a day in the yard the herd looked years older. Huge bulls died of stress and heart failure. Before the light came the stock workers were up to drive the weary herd from the yard to the station turkey. It wasn't far, but the heat and slow pace of flagging cattle led to a long day's work.

At breakfast Davie was adamant the journey was doomed. "Give 'em a spell at the yard, eh," he was saying to Greg as Susan slipped into the bunk-house kitchen. "Them cattle's all crook from musterin' when you do it from the air, chopper job, they run too fast. They're parched, they 'ad no feed or water, they'll starve. You gotta leave 'em a few days, fatten 'em up, then they'll be right."

"Yeah," added Pete, "today we should fix that windmill, the yard tank's near empty, an' the oil wasn't changed after the wet."

Greg shunned their advice, compounding the decline.

In the dingy bunk-house kitchen Davie collected billy cans,

mugs, powdered milk, sugar and a sugar-encrusted spoon, white sliced bread, a handful of salt in a twist of plastic, bundles of rib bones and such rations all neatly packed in the cardboard tucker box for smoko and cut lunch.

Below the dawn star he walked from the kitchen block, misty breath puffing before him. Davie was seething inside. He knew that Greg Palmer mustered from the air because he didn't know the bush. Davie could neither read nor write – working with the cattle had been education enough.

At first light he and Susan went to the corral. The bay mare whinnied, nodding agreeably as the stockman approached. Davie ducked between the wooden rails, greeting the mare, caught hold of her forelock, rubbed the white blaze, then patted her brown neck, under the tousled black mane.

Susan went on to all fours, crept on stony red earth beneath the lowest rail to stand alongside Davie. Over the hills the dawn glow diluted the deep blue sky with a watery yellow hue, Susan could see a lone brown mare on the far side of the corral, dozing. She screwed up her eyes, wishing her gun horse would come to her, or at least that she could catch the horse single-handed.

Davie stooped over, tapping down the back of the bay mare's knee to the fetlock. She was a good-tempered stock horse that Davie had chosen with careful selection: light, strong, hardy; a proud carriage of head, long, fine neck, well-sloped shoulders, level back, clean legs to cover plenty of ground. The mare picked up a foot, he rested the wall of the hoof in one hand.

Davie examined the mare's shoes, mumbling to Susan about the past when there were no night paddocks, but there was always someone to tail horses and mules; in those days the horse tailers took first night watch.

"We used to mother 'em up slow like, then cattle'll settle fer night watch, y'know. Then there were plenty men."

Davie decided that it was time the mare was shod, let the hoof down, went to her hindquarters, stroked his hand round the firm

56

reddish-brown flank, checking the hock and back tendons for swelling. The bay mare made long lips that reached affectionately for the shirt on Davie's stomach, and snapped only air. Davie stroked the withers, the mare looked on patiently while he spoke to Susan.

"Things're bad 'ere, you'll see. That Looma mob, they was replaced by white cowboys. Pete an' Rikki is the only ones left."

Susan studied the stockman with pensive, inquiring eyes. "Why do you stay here, Davie?"

"Me?" Davie glanced at her. "Don't know, don't know anythin' else." Davie ducked back between the rails, Susan mirrored his movements. He leant against the corral fence, gazing at rolling cloud banks in the sky. "Bin 'ere all me life in this country 'ere, never bin to a city, not even Perth. My brothers and sisters were sent south to Perth, I've not seen them since then."

Susan felt very close to Davie, the words he had spoken had struck a chord. "But you could leave, couldn't you?"

Davie didn't answer. Susan couldn't think of anything to say, she walked alongside him as he went to sort leather carriers for the pack horse.

The ringers rallied in the station corral to catch horses and saddle up under the low light of morning.

When every gun horse was tacked up and the pack horse tied at the corral fence, Davie and Susan returned. Their horses were next to each other, the reins knotted about the pommel.

Davie went to load the pack horse, protectively pushing Susan back lest the horse kicked. Susan held the bridle for him while he tightened the surcingle, listening intently to each word he said.

"See, I was too young when taken from my family at that station to 'member them first years at that Catholic mission. Beagle Bay, the mission there." Yet he remembered grandfather, and his mother. Hers was a blind faith. She had cooked, cleaned and fetched water from the river for the station homestead at Mistake Creek.

57

Davie gave Susan a reflective look, and slumped his body to one side. He remembered his last days at the mission well; when parsons loomed from the pulpit he shrank from holy windows with Christ upon the cross. The best part of his childhood, he contemplated, had been wasted, singing through hymns with uninhibited gusto; Davie had been deprived of the old lore. "Assimilation, I think they called it – said it'd 'elp with integration. Given the choice I'd've stayed on that station, but we bedda go now, sun's up, see," said Davie. Sliding his hand under the pack horse's belly, he took care to ensure that the surcingle wasn't too tight. The pack horse breathed heavily, so did Davie, to let the past go.

Susan untied the reins from the pommel of her mare's saddle, put her foot in the stirrup iron and hopped, grasping the pommel for aid, scrabbling into the saddle as Davie gave her a leg-up and the gun horse began ambling away.

Mounting his mare, Davie continued. "There weren't many white women on the stations then. Some of my family were already married, or promised to their own people, but the kartiya didn't care."

Again, Susan felt very close to Davie. He turned his mare from the corral, the pack horse in tow, and he and Susan rode level with each other, heading after the ringers, trotting cross-country over waving prairie; their line of sight, the blue canyon.

Upon reaching the yard fence Davie branched off; one after another the ringers followed, stopping briefly at the watering trough. The stock workers complacently filed into the yard, mingling in a disturbed sea of horned heads, pitching and tossing. From the holding pen they moved briskly. Rikki opened the gate, Greg rode ahead, the leader bull picked up his trail, and the white ringers formed a ring about the herd to prevent saucy steers, cows and calves from breaking into the bush. Davie's mob secured the rear, shepherd-like, encouraging young ones on as they gently wrangled around cattle, trooping them out in the standard formation for droving.

Soon the sun was high, its searing eminence portentous of an ever-lasting ride on the warped cord of red sand track, banked with ever-green bushes dividing the grasslands. As the heat increased, their guard slackened around cattle, lame from want of stamina. Piercing sun rays filtered through the suave wing-span of a circling hawk's glide and urgency set in; there was no time for smoko; they forced the wretched beasts to hasten, pushing them onward to water before they collapsed.

The wheeling predator cleared the solar blaze for blue as the track rose, petering out in a sandy area of dwarfed bushes broken by a cool eucalyptus stand, sprouting from seminal tussocks of grasses.

Pete called to Davie, "Them cows're tonguin', we should pull up a while, eh?"

"'Ere we should rest, ay," said Davie, "give th'cattle a feed." After looking for agreement he rocked forward and, in a single movement, motivated the bay to canter. A lather of sweat drenched the mare's chest and neck, she scattered froth and slippery foam; snorting, she chomped at the bit as Davie skirted the herd and ringers to advise Greg of his decision.

Gradually they halted. Ray untucked the pouch in his canvas saddle bag and teased out a pear-shaped flagon, on foot he passed the vessel round. The warm, syrupy water lubricated dust-choked throats and quenched thirsty bodies.

In implacable heat the cattle wouldn't tarry for a feed. When he resumed the lead, the herd was reluctant to follow Greg; some dispersed, dissolving in thickly tangled bush. They must have lost a few then, in some shape the stock workers set off downhill, tailing three hundred thirsty beasts to a large, flat basin, arid with niggardly brown bushes and one soaring white-trunked eucalyptus, whose delicate contours primed the pale sky's quiescence with shining leaves creased green. Here the grasses grew in hummocks like a bumpy, downy field of newly scythed hay. Each hump, deceptive in its softness, hid a hard mound of the earth's crust.

A bedraggled calf strayed from the herd, he stumbled on a hummock, spindly legs crumpling like a drunk's.

Moving her horse towards the animal, Susan was perturbed.

"Leave 'im," said Davie. "'E best there. Too tired to walk. We 'ain't got time to stop again. Only one calf gone anyways."

"Hey, Davie! Hey!" exclaimed Rikki, pointing at three more wandering, tripping calves.

Davie trotted to them, dismounted in a dusty explosion and turned to shake the powder from his hair. Normally calves would take to the game at such an arrival, cutting skittish capers with their tails erect; these three blundered on a miserable excursion. Davie goaded, lightly shoving one. It was useless.

Undeterred by calls of dismay and besieging horses, all about them cattle rambled, cattle roamed, their dehydrated bodies panting rapidly as each slack jaw dribbled dewy-red cobwebs of blood to the ground.

Davie said he had never seen anything like that before. "This no good. Cruel, y'know." He decided to deliver the news to Greg and lurched forward, once more spurring the bay to canter. The worst was yet to come.

A small group of calves huddled under the chequered umbrage of a bush, their open mouths drooling translucent sinews threaded with sun. Curious at their appearance, Susan rode up and quietly dismounted; the sharp crack of a whip, then Greg Palmer swung down from his horse, handed Susan the tired whip and reins and barged past, saying, as he scoured over-grazed plain, that he needed something sharp to pierce the weaker part of the skull.

"If you hit the right spot it kills 'em instantly, saves 'em from a slow death." Susan offered her penknife. Greg bowled a feeble calf down, straddled it, raised a hand high, and clumsily plunged the blade deep behind an ear. Spasms of shock shook through the pathetic frame, kicking legs resisted and retracted. Greg stabbed below the jaw, pumping the knife into the calf's fleecy neck. Frantic eyes rolled lime-white back on themselves in the throes of the creature's convulsions; a hoarse bleat rose through the hot air, its nostrils furiously blew blooded bubbles of dust. Jabbing at the gory crown, Greg uncorked bloody jets which oozed back to creamy fur. When he skewered the hollow temple above an eye, Susan averted her gaze, but her ears pursued the gruesome sounds as he wrenched and screwed the dead head off.

The afternoon wore on. Greg didn't know what he was doing and could not stop. Susan lingered queasily in his shadow, wondering which 'spot' was the right one, and why he bothered, for the longer he pursued with his barbaric execution, the more rasping cattle perished.

With arms and hands imbrued with gore, Greg slew all the calves of that congregation. Gaping lesions marred their heads and blood congealed on carrion corpses, once alive to the quick, now biotic in flies. Sufficed, Greg grunted, and straightened; his hair streaked with the slaughter, the starched shirt dappled soggy.

Davie dragged the lacerated carcasses to rest on the fallen paper-skin of the gigantic eucalyptus. Raw strips of bark peeled and flaked up to the cleft fork of the highest bough's ample armpits, around the roots a mass of ashy leaves lay, swept by the wind like weed with the tide; in this shroud Davie entombed the bodies.

The heat had subsided. Greg seemed detached, he reached for his reins. All mounted, looking to the scattered herd. Solitary cows loured, their fevered heads drooped, towing a thin slimy line of saliva, or they mooched in small groups, sullen under trees.

Davie's tone was blunt. "Never seen anythin' like this before, too many cattle crook 'ere. Best head back to the station, bin 'ere long enough." Greg glowered intimidatingly. "Only a suggestion," sighed Davie in contrition.

61

"Yup," retorted Greg, "these mongrel beasts're a waste a time."

From the saddle Davie rolled a cigarette. As he lit it, he flinched. He reined his mare past the calves' splintered skulls hidden by foliage, towards the few remaining cattle, suffering in shade.

Susan rode behind Davie, watching his back move in time with the horse. His shoulders looked weighed down like a well-worn bridge between bygone days and modern ways, his status had been reduced to that of a peon. Susan remembered the night of Greg's arrival: the cowboys, the cattle man, clinging to the old times, bringing in the new.

The estranged, depleted herd was a sorrowful parade on High Rocky's shimmering horizon. Dazed horses highlighted in the afternoon's henna hue, necks outstretched, heads shamefully low, ears loosely flopping to every plod; smelling strongly and warmly, soaked in sweat on sweat. When they neared the last barren stretch of wasteland before the homestead, the steady pace they had achieved was disrupted. The cattle smelt water and launched into a canter. Greg hailed "Whoa!" from his restless horse in an attempt to buffer the stampede's current; his command was drowned as a fierce army of cloven hooves streamed through rearing dust. Davie's mob, traumatised by the day's events, trailed in disarray.

One ringer galloped ahead to open the station gate. The herd poured past, careering through the turkey fence they broke up the soft, steep bank, floundered to the summit, gushing out of sight, swarming down into the dam.

Curtains of cloud scumbled the sunset and all were frail from hustling the herd out of the turkey dam and restringing dismantled segments of the barbed wire fence.

By sundown Bill Roberts, the manager, sat under the back porch of the station house, eating stew. Greg's ringers and Davie's mob ate together at the black table in the kitchen block, then Bill entered with a smirk as dirty as the cattle dung that fell from the tread marks of his boots to soil the shining floor.

"G'day mates. Hows ya doin'? Stand in a line, I wanna 'ave a good look at yous all." At this address they left their meal and filed along the metal sideboards. The manager clumped to and fro, blatantly smirching manure over polished tiles. "I shot a lazy horse from under a man once, blasted 'is brains out. That's the kinda man I am, that's the kinda man I wanna be 'n' that's the kinda man I wants workin' fer me."

Davie, playing on Bill's words, nudged Susan, whispering, "Don't know what 'is problem is, 'e ain't drunk." To contain her countenance, Susan kept her sight to the floor, happy to be by Davie's side.

"One of yous has the upper hand over the resta you mob, knows how I am to be treated." Sternly back and forth, Bill lustfully scrutinised his workforce, hating each in turn. They waited for the bomb to drop. "*God!*" he roared. The row of ringers jumped stupendously. "That's how you should treat me. What am I?"

There was a demure pause. No one dared move. A bluebottle flitted against the gauze-shielded window, the whining buzz from the snared insect jarred with the manager's confident nasal twang.

In a sudden surge of hatred came Bill's outcry. "I create the goddam work for yous all, keeps you fed, gives yous grog 'n' that. If any one of you mob doesn't toe the line you'll be out. Since I arrived many have been permanently rejected from this place an' there'll be more. Fer any of you who don't know English that means sacked, okay, 'cos I ain't feedin' you lazy cunts-fer-nothin'."

The bluebottle's wings were shredding in the shield's perforations, its fight for freedom distracted Bill. He squished the insect into the gauze, rubbing gummy mucus on a rolled-up shirt-sleeve. "There's been a lot of changes 'ere an' there'll be more. Greg does

63

a good job, some of you ringers don't an' I ain't 'avin' that. There's been trouble-makers 'n' ringers leavin' left right an' centre an' I ain't 'avin' that. I tell yous when to come, I tell yous when to go. Mark my word, some of your days are numbered on my planet."

Breathing down their necks, Bill Roberts walked back along the row of workers, then left them riveted.

Davie wouldn't let Susan wash up after the meal; he said she had best go have a shower and rest, escorting her to the bunk-house, insisting she best get an early night.

In the bunk-house corridor was a gang of rowdy white youths, newly arrived from Queensland. Susan made her way through them to her room, fearing they might be there to replace Pete, Rikki, Davie and herself. The notion incensed Susan so dreadfully she couldn't find the words to mention it to Davie.

Davie knelt down amidst a barrage of youths' legs to roll up his swag on red tiles. Susan watched with interest at the entrance to her room, and asked where he was going.

"Me? I'm jus' movin', that's all."

"Where?"

"Not far. Campin' out tonight. You stay."

A lump rose in Susan's throat. "Where are you camping?"

"Round the turkey, takin' the blue dog, one from that caravan. Gotta watch them cattle, night watch, see they might break through that fence again. Them ringers didn't mend that fence proper." Davie paused, struggling with swag straps. "Me, I can put th'bleedin' things up. Can't even mend a bust fence, that mob, don't know what's wrong wi' 'em." Davie, kneeling up on one knee, buckled the swag straps. He was ready. "Don't go doublin' up with these new cowboys, don't let 'em in yer room."

Susan went numb. Davie paused, looking round at the girl, he felt bad about leaving her. "You'll be right 'ere on yer own."

Later they passed each other by the spin-dryer in the flooded laundry, furbished with evening light.

"Made me jump," yelped Davie, side-stepping a swamp of blue denims. He gathered his clothes, Susan followed his movements imploringly. "What's up? You wanna come, you wanna camp out?" There was no need to answer. "Come on then. Fetch yer swag, you gotta be quick. Real quick. Yuh hear me?"

They built four fires around the turkey fence to ward cattle from the wire, and gathered a stock of wood piled high to last until daybreak. Although well watered, the cattle wouldn't quieten; moaning and bellowing, hungrily they churned up the little paddock limiting the grasslands.

At nightfall Greg drew up in a jeep alongside the fire where Davie and Susan had their camp.

The ringers slept anyhow, sprawled on swags; their empty cans littered a strip of plain where the stubble was trodden flat. Stars were strung faint and far. The Milky Way a motionless film of pearly lace collaring the vaulted dignity of darkness.

Susan lay down on her bedding roll; shaking with fatigue, she rested her head on her hands. She was too troubled to sleep, so watched a flame's jig cheaply lighten Greg's pert, waxen face. His head lolled back, exposing the adam's apple; to the violent tune of lowing cattle, he snored upright in the front seat.

In a bed of charred-ochre grasses, Davie was couched on his swag, his whiskers lit by fiery announcements, straw-coloured hair relieving the creased forehead, falling back to calumet grasses. Null eyelids were folded down, lips fell open, brown hands with open palms curled fingers at his side, and he too snored freely with the cattle's rhapsody and the night noises of which they were all a part.

Pete and Rikki, the blue dog at their heels, trudged back and forth fuelling fires, checking fences long into the night. The blue dog barked when the men passed the jeep, it must have woken Greg. He called to them in the gruff voice of disrupted slumber.

"Hey, over here."

Pete and Rikki clambered into the jeep to sit side by side on the passenger seat. What little their faltering tones had to say and the clatter of Greg's tongue were outlawed by the boastful huffs of cattle.

Susan saw Rikki approach. Behind him a bright star sketched on a blank sheet of sky as it fell. Rikki crouched down beside Susan, speaking quietly.

"The manager say we gotta leave on Friday."

Susan asked why.

"That's all Greg Palmer said."

"What do you think though? We work hard."

"That's all 'e said."

Susan rotated her wrist-watch to survey its veiled face until caught by the flickering fire. It *was* Friday, 2.30 a.m. Susan was dumbfounded.

Rikki and Pete disappeared into darkness, spluttering flames died, the beasts' bellows were dampened in a funeral of blackness. There was no moon. Another star drew a smooth arc. It was the coldest part of night.

Greg slept. Feeling so far from that cowboy's company, Susan stealthily eased herself from the swag, aware only that her mob, and this cattle station, was gone. She cradled batches of wood from the stack to stoke ruddled embers. All night she toiled while four fires furiously crackled, mocking a smouldering rage.

The morning's darkness wiped chilled cheeks, lifted; sleeping bodies stirred on swags. Susan crept back to Davie's camp.

Davie awoke, rolled over in his swag, raised his head and saw Susan's thoughtful eyes. She sat close by on the crinkled grass, her knees tucked in against her breast.

Davie rubbed his cold nose, shook grassy locks, sitting up, he folded back swag flaps. Feeling like he had been rudely stripped of everything from his bed he yawned. "You know? Couldn't tell you meself. Greg told me last night. 'E's 'ead stockman now, see, we gotta do as 'e says."

Susan looked away, half whining as though wrongly accused

of breaking the law. "Why, Davie? We work hard. They shouldn't sack any of us. We've done no harm, we haven't done anything wrong."

"They got them boys 'ere, friends of Greg's, from 'is school in Queensland."

The sun was rising over the plain. Susan stood, and turned her back on Davie, with the light her face changed colour to fiery autumnal copper. Her eyes stared into the scarlet sky. "They're going to replace us with these boys."

The stockman arose, buttoned his shirt and pulled up crumpled overalls. To hide the wizened look of being erased, Davie packed bedding rolls. "I don't know, Bill says they're experienced ringers. It's not up to me, it's up to 'im 'n' Greg. Couldn't even tell you last night. I wouldn't do this, you know that. You know that, don't you?"

The stockman looked her in the eye, in his was a sadder sigh. Susan was shattered. For a while they stood weak-kneed with despair, energy sapped to the ground.

A line of galah decorated the top poles of the corral. Pink-breasted from the rising sun, they waited for an excuse to take flight.

"Gotta pack up yer things now," said Davie. "We'll be back in town soon, Pete, Rikki, me 'n' you." Davie's tone hardened. "A man can't work in a place like this, bleedin' 'opeless 'ere. You saw them cattle yesterday. Head stockman. I'm not like that, y'know. Never seen anythin' like this."

A tear escaped from Susan's eye, hitting the ground. With it Davie spat out some disgust – a signal: birds took to the air in a deafening chorus, soaring in squadrons above.

"Greg, 'e's new 'ere, that's all. I'll put this right. I was 'ead stockman 'fore 'e came. You wait 'ere, I'd best see Bill Roberts."

Susan felt too tiny to move anything, effaced by the reddening sun. A deluge of red earth seemed to be sucking her in, red-eyed with a belly of brimstone that flamed and burned her up. Everything looked red and raw. The red wasn't hot, it was cold; a cold, white red.

Davie walked back red in the sun. Speaking gently now, he slowly shook his head. "One more day. One more day for Pete 'n' Rikki to sort their things out, but you go back to Derby. As fer me, I don't know." He smiled, vaguely triumphant at having won a day.

The stockman bypassed the kitchen and breakfast and strolled out to the corral. Susan followed blindly. The defiant flock swooped back on them, screeching a raucous furore of protestation.

When Davie reached the wooden fence his bay mare saw him, whinnied, and trotted across the red dirt corral towards him. Susan crawled under the fence and went to say goodbye to the brown mare. The sun began to warm Davie's shoulders, he watched Susan walk away, and with his mare, felt very alone.

Susan's mare stood apart from the herd; in the morning light her dark coat shone. Susan put her hand out, the mare gave it a welcome sniff with her soft dark muzzle, and her ears twitched forward. Susan stroked the withers, the hair felt rough and warm; she put her arms around the arched neck and tears flowed with the mane. They had been a long time coming.

Davie stalked up behind Susan, sheltering her with soothing words. "Don't cry now. We'll find you back in town soon. Don't forget yer pay now, 'e ain't 'avin' us fer nothin'. We'll find you, we'll work someplace else, Pete 'n' Rikki, me 'n' you."

Davie didn't want to leave the girl. In silence with her, there was sweetness in such a bitter moment.

When she turned, the stockman had gone. Susan felt pain and wished she had said goodbye. Davie had been – well, he was – everything to her, but she couldn't put it into words. It was like she was meant to be there, and life had felt new. She had felt new. And now she was lost again. Thrown back into confusion. Life was a blur and her head went heavy.

ONE OF THE RINGERS drove Susan back to Derby across the arid plain. The journey went quickly. They passed upturned carcasses of cattle whose bellies full of swollen gases, out of all proportion, belied their starved stomachs, and Susan felt empty.

A body called Susan sloped into town. She had no particular desire to do anything. She wasn't depressed, just suffering a catastrophic loss. A loss of something she had never had before; something she desperately needed. A loss of something that freed her spirit. The loss of a feeling of belonging.

She hung around in the heat with nowhere to go and nothing to do and chanced upon a bereft drover. He sat cross-legged on the pavement, his bare feet bloated, the bruised black skin and bone bandaged in rags. From under his wide-rimmed hat, eyelashes sheltered red round eyes – too drunk to see. The man was reaching out; he only wanted a dollar or two. Susan paid up and followed him. Derby had two main streets, both straight and parallel, one had most of the shops, the other a hospital, post office, hotels and banks. There were about five pubs, each carrying a sign on the door listing all the No's. No Hats, No Casual Clothes, No Customers Without Shoes – to keep the majority of the population out. Most of the shops sold liquor, all the hotels did. The drover staked the dollars at the TAB then drank outside on the streets.

This exile, camouflaged under the crude shade of a fat boab, sprawled on grass verges in a stupor; or sat on the springy sprinkled grass strip of fresh green dividing that alien road. The situation was bizarre: the drover supported this town in his state; the pubs, hotels and shops.

Sweaty booze oozed shame's sickly stench in the humidity. Susan could smell it from a few metres away; smell the destruction buildings offered as he cuddled the railings on the post office ramp or went lamp post leaning. A hot wind blew by mid-afternoon as she traipsed through the outskirts of Derby, following him to the black side of town, of campfires out back, mattresses in sand, plastic chairs and a whole heap of dogs. She watched the clean streak of a white van's sweep, wire laced black with fingertips clinging to imported justice. The police scooped up a group, "dumped 'em in a cell, dried 'em out fer-a-couple-a days 'n' nights. We charge 'em thirty dollars, they'll be right." And the hectic world of sun-cream, fluorescent surf wear and inexpensive smiles prospered on the parameters, turning a blind eye behind reflective sun-glasses.

Town dogs howled at the sun's farewell, clouds brushed streets with rushing black shadows. Susan looked up at a heavy grey sky. It was going to rain.

She had booked in at the hostel, it was pleasant, fourteen dollars a night for full board.

Against torrential rain Susan sprinted along Clarendon Street to the Spinifex Inn. Out of breath, she ordered a drink. Her sight swept across the oblong-shaped saloon as she skinned off the wringing wet blue anorak: the small round wooden tables stained mahogany dark, matching chairs set slightly apart, the games table, a juke-box kept quiet at one end of the room. The saloon was empty but for two elderly men seated at the bar, clad in smart grey suits, their shoulders darkened, dripping. As though it were impolite not to do so, they jovially included her in their conversation.

"Lovely weather for ducks. You speak English, do you? And where are you from?"

"England," said Susan, wiping water from her face.

"Nurse, are you?"

"No, I'm a student, from Bristol, on a working holiday."

"Don't look much like a Bristolian to me. We're English, you see."

"Looks more African to me," said the other man. "I say, you look more African. Where were you born?"

"London."

"Which part of Africa are you from? You see, I've worked overseas most of my life. Spent many years in Africa, off the Ivory Coast, you know."

Susan staggered through explaining that her home was now Cornwall and she had lived in Hampshire for most of her life.

"Well, I'd say she's ... possibly from Sierra Leone. You could be from Sierra Leone. Where are your parents from?"

"I don't know," replied Susan.

"Oh. Here, another for the girl. What are you drinking? What was it?"

"No, no, thank you," said Susan. "I'm fine as I am."

"You could be from Ghana, they're dark there."

"Barman, another for the girl. What's your name?"

"Susan."

"Susan, what will you have?"

"No, honestly."

"How long did you say you'd been in London?"

"Bristol."

"But you were born in London. She said she was born in London!"

"From her accent you can tell." The men either side of Susan converged to debate her origins, each word was like an incisive

71

rod, cutting. "I think the features are more like the Central African's. You know, the nose, forehead. Are you sure you're not from Chad?"

"Rhodesia. That's it!"

"No, no. I'll bet she's Ghanaian, west coast. Tell a lie, Nigerian."

Susan felt unworldly and transparent. The answer to their question was quite simple, "The Caribbean," but she had only been there twice. She remained silent.

The men turned, engaged in conversation, Susan listened to the exchange.

"You know, they're all the same, every single one is tarred with the same brush. They might hold a job for a few weeks, but you know, they're just not as clever."

"It's been proven with scientific tests, they don't have the same amount of intelligence, their brains *are* smaller, and it's my opinion, there's less in them."

Feeling like an inartistic ornament the men had picked up out of curiosity, spurned, and plonked down for junk, Susan went to sit on her own.

Outside rain pelted on the corrugated iron roof of the inn, it streamed along gutters, splashing round the doorway, drowning the whine of brakes as a coach pulled up in the parking bay. The weary coach party entered the saloon bar, filling the air with chatter from their tour of the Kimberley as they bought drinks and gradually dispersed to the wooden tables dotted about the room.

A sharp woman's voice sliced through Susan. "No, I'm not going near her to get that paper." The woman referred to the *Sunday Age*, a popular Melbourne street paper, on the adjacent seat. Susan was smartly dressed, the mauve frock becoming on her agile body, and guessed it was because she was black. Susan remembered her parents, who would benignly say, "Colour doesn't matter, everyone's equal," yet, to her great surprise, when she stepped outside their integral warmth, it seemed to matter terribly. She thought of Hampshire where she was raised, a county short in cultural diversity; the family, blind to racial

72

inequality, never associated with other black people, and so Susan learned to be the odd one out.

As a young child she fantasised she was a distinguished princess in her ivory tower, who might be whisked, in a primitive way, to a mysterious darkness. Occasionally her parents had taken her to London. These trips excited Susan: she was intensely intrigued at sighting another black. When she spotted one she would skip behind her mother's skirt in hiding, or superstitiously grip her father's hand as he strode, inadvertent, along city pavements.

Once in a blue moon an Afro-Caribbean theatre company toured the New Forest: Susan had thought it perverse to watch these thespians perform their blues, or comic for an audience whose opulence and ignominious ways had stolen their ancestral rights. She sipped at the beer. In her mind's eye, Susan saw the girls who had been her closest childhood companions: sisters from a military family who lived in a mansion with battlements, a monkey puzzle tree on the front lawn where at full mast a Union Jack keenly flapped; "Whiteways" was inscribed on the copper name plate of the long gravel drive. She pictured Janice in her bedroom, routinely raking through a vanity case brimming with cosmetics designed for fair skin; her sister Belinda, posing in a mirror with ringlets that coiled down her creamy-white neck. She on a bed behind with an embarrassingly unfading brand, frizzy wire-wool hair that seemed to lend itself as much to styling as an old man's beard. In her reflective frame of mind, Susan saw the ugly duckling she was, remembering that at school she had been in an ethnic minority of one, and when she arrived, the number of white pupils decreased. She had become accustomed to narrow, stereotypical concepts about her race – all of which were derogatory. Her classmates, who couldn't string together a constructive sentence to support her struggle, even if they'd wanted to, developed their parents' staunch conservative attitudes.

A little princess had grown into a disenchanted teenager who resented her privileged upbringing; the importance of material

73

possessions and mock sophistication that were the free-spending middle-class norm; yet there was no comfort in the abhorrent baseness of the lower class, whose scum she feared might infect her, and the upper-class niceties and affluent worldliness, she couldn't break through. Above all else, Susan had envied her family's comparative white ease.

She observed the newspaper, picked it up; the print was soggy from the downpour, leaving a patch of condensation on the chair. Unfolding the paper she saw a photograph enclosing smudged grey figures, grey faces, reminding her of walking through the suburbs of Melbourne, the rainy scent of the seaside city where she had received a mixed reaction: wide berths, anxious glances. A group of white youths had jeered, stood in her path, her heart missed a beat, she dodged through. Graffiti on a factory wall claimed one of Australia's underlying problems: "50,000 Years of Culture, 200 Years of Plunder." These words had haunted her during the walk: passing the McDonalds Centre and play park, public barbecues made of new red brick that took ten cents, open kiosks on the promenade every hundred yards, sewage, litter, empty cans of Foster's everywhere, "No Dogs On Beach" signs in between the kiosks; Murdoch newspapers, the huge incinerator, the Melbourne skyline – grey, surreal, impermanent.

She glanced over her shoulder at the bar. The Englishmen hadn't gone. The man behind yarned about bullfrogs in The Territory. "Australia is constantly overrun by one species or another. Epidemics of toads, donkeys, rabbits, each region has its affliction." It seemed paradoxical to travel to the antipodes, now mixed in nationality and culture. Yet the majority of the population originated from Europe, many of their ancestors being rejects of a cruel mother country – the poverty stricken and criminals of Britain. Unlikely qualifications for residency in either country nowadays, thought Susan. She folded the newspaper back on the chair as two portly men entered the inn, dressed in white shirts and khaki shorts, knee-high socks sheathing stumpy legs furred in ginger hair. The first man leant back against the bar to smooth talk his introduction to the coach party in a singsong drawl.

"G'day, I'm yer new driver, Ron, an' me mate Al will be takin' over later. We'll be leavin' Derby in …" His sight bent down to read the digital wrist-watch winking a prompt. "… an hour an' a 'arf or so, an' we'll be drivin' 'cross the desert s'far as Alice Springs. On the way we'll be stoppin', uhh, roughly every two to three hours, then again at Alice, that's a long stop, mind you, so yous can get a lotta beers in. An' late afternoon we'll always be stoppin' fer tea."

Another man's voice. "And crumpet." A laugh.

"Hey, where's this crumpet?" replied the driver, leering round the saloon. "Yer right. Yer can't 'ave yer tea without crumpet, eh."

A cold draught glided through the air. From the tables around her Susan overheard fragments of conversations: "So you're a McCormick. I knew the McCormicks, they came in 19 …", "And you were from the Fraser family – you know, my sister married a Fraser and he was a Liberal too." The nebulous ghost of the White Australia Policy seemed to echo the fragility of the predominant cultural structure with its European prevalence, and the desire to find security by identifying with its progenitors. Susan sat, dwelling on parallel insecurities … the dutiful move to Brixton, where she couldn't understand the Caribbean lingo and the Rastafarians she latched on to had found the articulate enunciation, acquired from elocution classes, and her unfamiliarity with Black history bad form, or at best entertaining. It had been a fruitless upheaval: their consensus concluded that, having been brought up in the enemy camp, Susan was a fake – a semblance to the coconuts on sale in Brixton market: black on the outside, white on the inside. When with these people, that was exactly how she felt.

Disillusioned, Susan spun the ashtray on the table, deliberating

75

that it was not her colour that had made her forlorn, it was the consequences.

A small crowd had gathered around the juke-box at the far end of the saloon, amongst them a Tasmanian art student, adorned in hippy memorabilia. He sauntered up to Susan, loudly introduced himself, pulled up a chair and sat down next to her. Water seeped from his hair, trickling in runlets down pallid pockmarked cheeks. Unprompted, he began venting hostilities about the native Australians and, once he got going, acrimony gushed.

Susan didn't want to talk. She lit a cigarette, smoke went in her eyes. She could hear that the rain had stopped. Her sight focused on the varnish of the round wooden table, plashed with droplets from the man.

Shafts of evening sun shone through broken clouds and her thoughts strayed to Davie, with whom she had felt unity. Filled with love, light and happiness she stood. Excusing herself, she gathered up the drenched coat draped on the back of the chair, banged her thigh on the corner of the table, and made it to the door – Susan never had been too good at saying what she felt inside.

She pushed the door open and stepped out on to the street. It was deserted. It was hot, humid, all day, all night, there was never a break from the stickiness. Susan paused. Music from the juke-box floated into the street, the words of the song, she could just pick them out: "… came from a town that was so small, look both ways you could see it all", which was true, Derby's streets were short. If she stood in the middle she could see open scrub at either end.

Susan stood, waiting for action to start. The big one. The shoot-out at sundown. It was an angry afternoon. She wanted a place that felt safe. Didn't know which way to go on the front line of that Wild West town. She felt closed up in darkness, seeing the setting sun. Her thoughts returned to Davie and she realised that she and Davie had barely mentioned their pasts and the under-

76

current they shared. She gazed across the street, reflecting on words he had said, then, checking loose change in her coat pocket, went to the pay phone to call him.

"Hello."

"Hello." There was an echo, Susan shook the receiver.

"G'day." It was a woman's voice.

"Hello. Is Davie there, please?"

"No. Look, he's a bit busy at the moment."

"I'm Susan, a friend of Davie's. We worked together at High Rocky, he gave me this number —"

"Yes," the woman interrupted, "I know. I'm Davie's girl-friend."

"Oh, sorry." Susan twisted the spiral cord to the receiver and voiced baffled thoughts. "I'm looking for work on the cattle stations and I wanted to ask whether he might know of anyone who needed anyone, or any work going. When will he be free?"

"I could give him a message." The woman sounded reluctant.

"Well, I guess you could say I rang."

"Okay. Goodbye."

Susan wondered why she had never known about the girl-friend. "Thank you. Goodbye." She returned the telephone receiver and meandered back in confusion to the noisy saloon bar.

In the cockshot light of the Spinifex Inn where anything could happen and nothing much did, Susan sat on a stool with her back to the bar and smoked. A dusky wisp of a figure emerged from a door at the far end of the room, Everette Owen, and behind, his woman, Marlene. They slid through shadows and soft sheets of sunlight past the games table, covered in jaundiced felt.

The art student hailed Susan to catch her eye. Susan didn't know what he wanted, nor did she care to find out. Snatching up the glass in her left hand, she silently slipped from the stool and sidled to the gaudy green glow of the juke-box. Her right finger slid down smoothly moulded glass, over a neon acid-emerald

77

glare mirrored in her eyes, looking for ... "God Must Be A Cowboy At Heart"; she hadn't heard that one before. She pressed two dollars into the juke-box slot.

"It's a farce talkin' 'bout Land Rights, we gotta right to the land." Marlene, a woman with a man's voice, lectured at the bar. A tough girl who had that sleazy look in her eye that fooled many. Her thrifty endearments had bought Everette's heart.

Susan's fist clouted the machine, coins dropped, and the juke-box began to sing. Above it, the voice of Marlene: "In '85 we were given the vote in local elections, but there was a campaign against us. They call us activists, them politicians in that Canberra bureaucracy."

Everette Owen approached Susan. "You that girl bin workin' with Davie."

Susan looked round. "Yes, that's right, I was."

"What's up, 'ad enough o' High Rocky?" Sarcastically Everette sniggered. "You can try Anna Plains where I bin. S'all trotting horses, off the track, that mob won't gallop, jus' trot real fast."

"Try Callum, 'e's got a contract at Sun Creek station," said a voice.

"Sun Creek?" said Susan, glancing at the man behind. It was a man with a tattoo and the beady eyes of a squirrel.

"Yeah, used to be Fairfield, out by the Leopold Range."

The woman's voice again. "You don't wanna see us elected, yet we built this cattle industry, we should be given an equal say."

"We should go back to spears 'n' stop usin' guns, eh?"

Everette Owen laughed. "Over-grazed topsoil, even that's eroded. Sod it." Empty talk. They had heard it before. The helicopters, airplanes and bull-buggies running in the cattle, the stations going into decline. Laughter echoed in his head. Removing the ban on alcohol and the equal wage system had had devastating effects on their lives. "There's too many stupid cowboys 'ere."

"Yeah, an' what good have you sown?" It was the man with a tattoo. "You've lost everything, including your sanity. At least my heart's in the right place."

"Yeah, but your head isn't. There was even talk of poisoning the birds."

A nervous, eerie, hysterical screech. The monster swallows her up. She could feel its belly laughing at her, laughing round her for thinking then of Davie. Susan finished the beer and walked to the washrooms, splashed water on her face. There might be work in Derby. Perhaps she'd get a job at a store; she saw her reflection in the splintered glimmer on the wall that passed as a looking glass – perhaps not. Through the few town people she had got to know she had seen tight communities split into sections, fragmenting into organisations, subsections, sucking, pumping like living organisms: all fighting for Land Rights, all in conflict with each other in a political can of worms. Returning to the bar, Susan felt more downhearted. The tattooed man had settled at a table with some tourists; Owen and his woman were now gone.

"Their blood runs in my veins," the barman airily announced, adding dismissively, "What the 'ell, there's 'ardly any of 'em left now."

The art student moved to the bar. "Most Aussies resent 'em cos the government gives 'em so much social, say for transport, then they cheat, buy a really cheap car an' loadsa grog. Car's smashed up within a week. One week!" He was delighted. "They're never educated, y'know. I think that if you'd shot all of 'em, other blacks would be treated okay."

"C'mon," the barman chipped in, "they'll clean yer car for a pack o'smokes."

"The real problem you Aussies have," spouted the student, "is that you didn't wipe the Abos out."

"Yes," grinned the barman. "Same again?"

"Thank you," said Susan. The student examined her with his eyes. Back in the white world she felt like an animal, caged as a public spectacle. What could she do on the edge, in the limelight? Scream if anyone else stared.

But we all fall foul of not being heard: in England they would say, "We'd like to know all about it, do tell us what it's really like." Being an obliging novelty, Susan had tried spilling her guts over a coffee table, a bar, the din of a party to a momentarily captive audience who, disregarding their *objet d'art's* bleeding heart, were distracted by a passing car, the waitresses' legs, and wandered to another subject – something about women taking life too seriously – remembering someone they *must* introduce her to before asking again, "What was it like to be the black sheep in your family?" – and Susan thought she had been telling them: her relinquished revelations were metamorphosed, defiled and rendered the prelude to a side-splitter.

The grinning barman wiped the bar top. "It's all right," he gleamed, winking at Susan, "I don't see you as black." Susan tried smiling, paid for the drink and went to sit at a table, wondering whether to cut losses, get the next available seat on a plane back to England, or stay with few friends, no work and little money.

Rain pattered on the iron roof. Susan watched the coach party in dribs and drabs abandon the steamy bar for a dank, dark outside. The Englishmen still hadn't gone. She stubbed out the cigarette, put on her sodden coat, walking to the door, shoved the door open and stared from the doorway.

Across darkness streaks of silver raindrops fell as the tourists prepared to depart. Towards the rear of the vehicle's body was a hold with a big flap that raised vertically. The coach captain and driver swung luggage into this chasm until it was full. The crowd around them, heads shielded with coats, divided into passengers who mounted steps, disappearing behind muddied glass, or their relatives, partners and mates, trying to locate familiar faces inside.

The wet coat was cold, making Susan damp around her neck. She felt a homeless sorrow and her cheeks were burning. She thought of the spring, of the flowers of Cornwall. How much she

80

missed them. The banks of the River Tamar were so very far away.

Tickets torn, cargo stowed, the hydraulic door's rubber sucked rubber, then the noble coach rolled from the parking bay, swishing down the highway.

Rain splattered on rooftops, gushing from gutters into roadside drains awash with red sand rubble. At the entrance to the inn a girl stared at the darkened street, the driving rain. It was a beastly evening. She darted from the doorway; felt she had to keep moving. Couldn't get a grip on anything, was running backwards, falling, crashing down but there was no ground. Where to drown unwanted feelings?

Susan ran down the street, dashing through puddles in pitch dark and pouring rain. She silently slipped away. She had lost her sight having flown to four continents in search of the place for which she yearned: where her identity would be accepted, not ostracised, challenged and judged in curious expectation. As Paddy put it: "You cut off from your roots, you go adrift."

One week in town was enough for Susan, she tried phoning Davie again to find out whether he knew of any station work. He said he would give it some thought and that Rikki and Pete were in the lock-up after a brawl at the Boab Inn. Davie said he had a contract mending fences and would meet her at the Boab Inn the following afternoon. She waited there for three hours. He didn't show, but it was then that Susan found Paddy once more.

Paddy and Susan walked through Derby to the salty smell of the sea. As a custodian of the land the old man's eyes – fierce, fearless and kind – confirmed his identity.

"They shot my people, Ngarinyin, in the early days of settlement. Ngarinyin also speared a few white men." Silhouetted on water, they strolled along the jetty, watched blood juice seep from a sun ball, stains sponged by clouds, slaked by rocks to the glinting sepia sea. Paddy talked truths in monochrome tones, colour diffused from the water, his voice lapped the twilight ebb. "I flew Spitfire in the Second World War," the elder was proud of this, "but my land's near 'ere, I'm from Ngarinyin country. I was taken to the coast, further south, near the estuary." He talked of his childhood, before he left Swan River. Susan listened attentively. "The main industry was making brooms, with rushes and bamboo from the river. Government rations helped us exist in Perth. That was once a tribal area."

Paddy's sunken face was dark. He held his head high, fixing his sight a great distance ahead. "River used to run straight, now it sweeps round. They dug a diversion, they used landfill, cutting down wattle and paperbark trees, all the bush land there." He was a visionary, he saw the river; at daybreak he had snuggled under kangaroo skin blankets, when trees were black against the sky, sun rising in the east. "Nangaroo, the sun, that's a woman, spirits came that way. They took everything else, but the spirit's still there, can't take the spirit away."

Then Susan watched, and as far as the eye could see, surrounded by sandy, swampy patches were the communities of the Swan River; living in huts built of tin, rusted iron, bags, a round rush roof. "Before the coming of the white man they used black boy rushes, quite warm and cosy in the winter."

Gulls flew up the estuary, crying. Swans fed in the deeper areas of the tidal flats, the sky cloud free, blue as the sea. Running down the foothills to salt water beaches was a boy, the sun struck the sand with a glare, the sea wind blew it everywhere, stinging his face and eyes. Amidst thick clumps of brown bull rush heads, he sat on a rock and cried.

A gull flew down to the rock, stood on one twiggy leg and spied him with first one eye, then the other. Losing its balance, feathers whipped by the breeze, the gull took to the air.

Paddy sat with watery eyes while the wind played with the water round the rocks. Clear, saline water where single strands of slimy weed transparently drifted downriver.

Further up was another camp: "Nyoongah we call all 'em people down south, Kalyun called the black swan clan. They'd all be related, or most 'long the banks 'ere, the people of the swans."

The boy strolled along the shore collecting small spiral shells; he wandered in a maze of waterways where trees came down to meet the river. Reflected on the rippling water was the sun, leaving a shoal of sparkling stars, blinding him momentarily. There were crabs, prawns, fish. There were hundreds and hundreds of birds. There were so many swans the river was black with them. "They grew together," said Paddy, "the people and the swans. But the people were moved to Guildford and Bassendean, pushed back when development began."

Bloated blowfish lay dead, sun-dried rotten. Seaweed lumps housed hermit crabs in shells misbegotten. It was the end of summer.

Cranes stalked the water's edge, ducks dredged with plover, oystercatchers ran from breaking waves, mussels washed over. There were craggy cliffs lined with trees round a cove, without the ruffle of a breeze Paddy stood, by water like a mirror. It was quiet there. He saw the ibis bird of mystical beauty, spoon bills sifting little plants and algae; shells buried themselves in wet sand. The beach crunched beneath his feet, cool to the water's edge; he sank his toes in wet sand, like one of those burying shells.

He swam across inland lakes, explored islands; the bulky mounds of sticks and reeds were their nests, and Paddy paddled in shallows, liquid-blue cruising where swans arched graceful black necks.

And he thought of their flight; sounds of wings skimming

83

swishing waves. Black wings beating, silky black feathers beat air, red bills rose as the sun sank in crimson lakes. At sundown, the mellow honk of a flock travelled high overhead from one sheet of water to another. Floating. Circling the steady air-stream of vulnerability. Delicately sailing a warm wind. Anticipating. Deliberately debating a new tack, glossy black backs glided over the estuary. And a turbulent sea below.

With the sigh of inshore breezes gulls settled their webbed feet on wet sand; trees' leaves were barely stirring, trunks gold in the sun. "Mongers Lake, where the swans are now, they made a rubbish tip there."

A plume of smoke changed the sky to black over the trotting track and cricket grounds. "Like a rash you discover when you're workin'. What can you do? Can't do nothin', you jus' gotta keep on while it's growin'."

The swans cried "bibho-bibho", leaving for freshwater lakes in the evening. Pelicans and night-herons glided grey over reed beds. Frogs, common in the brackish swamps, croaked. The mist curled up the river with the lone curlew's call.

Paddy and Susan trampled mudflats boxed and pressed in python ruffs undrained by waves long gone. He wasn't tired that night from travelling although it was nearly nine o'clock.

"Time," the elder said, "that's white man's chains. Brolga dancin', see 'em, see 'em dancin' crane." Under moonshine they watched white brolga arabesque their elegance on salt marshes and Susan thought of her pirouettes on formal floorboards, and of her hands clutching a wooden bar in a hall in Hampshire that preserved that antiquated smell of plimsolls and simmering cabbages like the primary school. The ballet teacher had snipped at her fledgeling wings, pleading that her *pliés* were too petite, her *pas de chat* too pronounced, and heaven forbid – Susan's big black bottom stuck out so much that it was a dark obscenity on a proverbial lake of prancing flaxen cygnets.

On waterlogged pipe-clay of wetland, the elder and Susan squelched and waddled as they wandered: you see, he seemed to understand, or know benevolently. "I call you cus, like cousin, you kin, like me."

He drove to the Boab Tree prison, jawing, scary night talking. "Women used to work them stations. That mob o' girls at Mowanjum, they'll tell you 'bout it. They could ride an' everythin'. Even done a bit of it meself." From this man an intrinsic warmth radiated, sparking all around him freely as bolting lambs and calves had run, springing, skipping, innocently ravaging his country. The elder's wisdom usually wound up repeating itself. "But you might be startin' tomorrow, eh, you'll be right, you gotta folla yer star."

SUSAN FOUND DAVIE at his girlfriend's place in the cool truth of morning. Her bungalow was on the edge of town: timber-built, raised off the ground on stilts, the white paintwork flaking, tinted sulphur-yellow. Leafy trees surrounded the compound creating a patched screen against the sun.

Christine sat in placidity mottled by shade on the porch steps, another black woman stood one step above, a swaddled baby cradled to her breast in fondly rocking arms. A couple of teenage girls, bodies leisurely folded over the porch rail, shyly emitted faint sounds into cupped hands; their angular, dusty-black stick arms and legs poked from threadbare calico dresses, the colour of buttermilk; heads together, ebony hair gleamed as one, softly falling forward. Susan introduced herself and asked for Davie. Christine's shrill screech split the serene scene.

"Davie! Davie! C'mon out, there's that girl 'ere t'see you."

Less abrasively to Susan. "'E's inside, works on Kimberley time." Another hoydenish squawk. "Davie!"

"I'm comin', I'm comin'." Vigorously grooming his crop of hardy-hay hair with both hands, through the open doorway out stumbled anguished Davie: covered in dust; violet-blue eyes piercing; his swollen face ruddy, belly chubby, full of beer.

Welcome tones greeted Susan. "Where you bin? You right? Never thought I'd see you again," sighed Davie, "... well, I didn't know." He shrugged, looking her up and down; the dark eyes, rich skin, she was all there. By the look of her she'd had a rough night too.

Susan hugged Davie. He was unsteady as he released her, hitched up his jeans, wobbled on his boots. "C'mon then, don't jus' stand there. You can come inside." He turned to his women: "She's right, she jus' lookin' for work. This is Christine, you've met 'er anyway. She can come in?" Davie inquired doubtfully. Gingerly Susan climbed the steps, smiling to Christine as she skirted her. Christine returned an unintelligible grunt and indefinable wink. The mothering woman turned for Susan to pass. Davie chaperoned Susan through the front door, and into a darkened hallway.

The drop in light induced a momentary dizziness in Susan, culminating in the impetus to burst into tears. Perhaps it was Davie's timely, customary intemperance, the pleasure of being with him again. Suppressing the emotion, Susan asked him why he hadn't honoured their arrangement the previous afternoon.

"Well, I was there," said Davie indignantly. He still looked anguished and the rare eyes probed. "I waited but you weren't there. Couldn't see you anywhere. Must've just missed you or summin', didn't get there till four, see. Must've been after four. Must've missed you. Good to see you," he said without much conviction.

"I didn't think much of Bill Roberts," said Susan.

"Noooooh," the stockman's enthused headshake endorsed, "terrible place that."

"What have you been doing, Davie?"

"Fencin', like I told you on the phone." He was as agitated as ever. "Bin fencin' wiv that Callum Hall."

Susan said she would like to work with them. Davie was amazed. "What, fencin'? I don't know. 'Ard work, see, an' ... the wire, you never done it before, not easy see. Long days, no breaks like at High Rocky an' ... the flies, in this heat. Hot out there, it is. You might not like it. You gotta be strong. You'd be better off in town. Well, why not stay 'ere, you can stay 'ere if you like, she won't mind," he gambled, "stay 'ere. One of us now." Davie moved to check whether it would be acceptable for Susan to stay.

Diverting the tack, she nipped in quickly. "I'll work hard. You know that." Davie's eyes conveyed intense speculative thought; he scanned the well-swept floor, his filthy boots. When he looked up he tensed, bristling as though the quandary inflicted woe. His spiel was a prudent torrent.

"Not up to me. Callum, Callum's me contract employer. I work fer 'im. You'll 'ave t' see Callum. Don't know if 'e needs anyone else. Can't work for me, I can't pay you. You need money?" Susan nodded. "Me too. You got money or what? Well, I 'aven't got any. You'll have to talk to Callum Hall. Anyway," he added with a disparaging shrug, "we leave tomorrow. Callum lives nearby, take you there if you want but it's not just 'im 'n' me, there's this kartiya, white fella from the Northern Territory comin'. Already three of us, see. Might not even be enough room in that modorcar." Davie's huge frame was already through the doorway. He briefly explained to Christine who was malignant as a broody swamp hen, craning her neck round to find fault.

"She lookin' fer work. Not up to me. I can't give 'er no job. Takin' 'er t' Callum's place. Well move, c'mon move." Christine begrudgingly sheared to one side, Davie squeezed down past the women. "A man can't even get outa the 'ouse, don't know what's wrong wiv this place," he jabbered. Christine blew an agnostic, accusing raspberry. Susan looked away shyly; nearly falling down the steps to keep up, she scampered like a terrier behind Davie's great strides.

Callum Hall's house was on the next block, the customary design: long, low, residing on wooden legs, peeling paintwork a smarting palette for the sun. An overgrown hedge enclosed the shrub-filled garden, and whittled sprays of ochre grass lined the sandy concrete drive.

Davie's footfall lost tempo. "Truck's gawn. 'E's not 'ere. Sophie's 'ere, see." He strode to the gauze-covered doorway, up wooden steps condemned with wear. Susan loitered on the edge of the driveway, shuffling her boots in the sand, wishing she could become invisible when Davie knocked and a woman came into view from the sombre interior; her features were vaguely recognisable. After few words, a gesture in Susan's direction, Davie returned.

"Callum gone to town. She'll tell 'im to come to my place. You best wait wiv me." They ambled back to Christine's bungalow. The woman with the baby had gone, Christine and the two girls remained.

Davie gave Susan a discreditable glance from the porch. "Wait 'ere with them women," he said drily as he walked inside. "Best place for you."

A yellow Toyota pulled up in the variegated light. Out stepped a lithe, swarthy figure in a yellow T-shirt, blue jeans and a stately black Akubra styled down. Christine called Davie with a vibrancy equalling that of Susan's arrival, got up and waltzed inside, the girls relinquished furtive conversations, tiptoeing after her. The man whistled as he walked, he took Christine's place on the steps. Davie was upon him in no time. "Callum!" he panted.

"Davie!" mimicked Callum gaily, lifting his bum off the step post-haste. "Shouldn't creep up on me like that, y'know." He nimbly repositioned his seat. "Made me jump, Davie, give me a heart attack 'n' I'm bruised from that fummin' rodeo. What's up anyways, Sophie says you passed by."

"Not me, she want to see you, she works good," eulogised Davie, ushering Susan forward, "works real good, she that Pommy girl, told you 'bout 'er anyway 'n' bein' at High Rocky."

Callum swivelled his spritely body at the waist to bring Davie and Susan into sight: one foot rested on the bottom step; one leg

90

was raised, bent double, a knee against his side; a brown eye squinting, a brown eye examining; a toothy grin beamed beneath the swanky hat's rim. Callum pivoted to his former position, then, reaching forward, scraped up a handful of sand.

"Yeah, Davie, you told me. What 'appened to Pete 'n' Rikki?"

"They went on the piss, 'ad a fight, police locked 'em up. She lookin' for work, wants to work wiv us, fencin'. I said it's not up to me, she gotta see you, see."

Callum contemplated, fascinated by the copper-coloured dirt trickling from his clenched fist to the ground. He released a shallow yawn, the black hat turned reticently from side to side, he stood down from the steps and arched his back, forcing the spine to curve with his hands, he rolled his head to turn his face to the moon – a plain marble in the cloudless blue sky. Callum strutted stodgily, ceremoniously tracing a small circuit in the sandy yard, repeatedly stretching stiff bow legs. Swinging his right arm three times, he alerted Davie to join him, and trundled towards the Toyota. Davie brushed by Susan. The men converged, faltering at the truck, Davie's defensive actions saying, "I don't know, I don't know," and pleading utter ignorance.

The sun's ethereal hues dabbled with the leaves above the bungalow. Susan leant her forearms on the porch rail, observed the men and pondered on the precariousness of life.

Davie headed back. "Callum want to talk to you, go an' see 'im, I done all I can." He touched Susan goodbye. "Come round later if y'like, I'll be 'ere."

Susan went to join Callum, who slammed the door shut as he bounced into the truck. His eyes and nose were clandestine under the brim of his hat; his accent pliably alternated from a North West Australian drawl to South Eastern English, the tenor tones had the easy-going ring of an affable rascal with charismatic charm.

"Hi, I'm pretty pushed for time jus' now, but you can come in the truck with me while I pick up provisions in town. You'll 'ave t'catch me while you can." Callum was endowed with a quizzical, childlike air. "Come on round the other side." He reached across the passenger seat to open the door. Susan got in, pulling the door to – it hadn't shut properly. She fought with the jammed catch, painfully aware that this wasn't having the desired effect. "You gotta slam that door." Susan tried again, but the door refused to open or close. "You gotta slam 'im real hard." Callum leant across her to open the door in preparation for what was clearly going to be one almighty yank. "Won't always open from the inside, this door, that's why the window's down most times." Susan put her arm out of the window, felt for the handle and released it. Taking care not to fall into her lap, Callum heaved the door to, then turned on the ignition. "So, you're wantin' work. You done fencin' before?" Susan shook her head. "Know how to tension wire? Ever used a drill to dig holes? A crowbar?" Susan felt foolish. Callum pulled up outside his house, they weren't going into town after all. "Well, we'll be workin' out near Leopold Range, at Sun Creek station. Campin' out. Davie or I'll have a spare swag for you."

"I've got a swag," said Susan, grateful for that.

"We-e-e-l-l ..." Callum's eyes maintained their purdah, the plummy ripe cheeks dimpled and swelled, his toggle of a nose dilated as the concise lips blossomed a smile. "We-e-e-l-l, we're leavin' after noon tomorrow. Got some new bloke comin' from the Northern Territory, don't know what 'e's like. You can work with me, see how ya go, take yer on for a week. See how strong you are before settlin' yer pay, but you should earn 'round fifty dollars a week. Get all yer tucker too. Bush tucker. You should be right, Davie says yer all right. You can have a week's worth startin' tomorrow. After that, see how you shape up." Callum's speech was very bubbly. "Dependin' on how you do we've got, say ..." He looked down at his pimento-brown hands resting on the black triangle of plastic seat between his legs, mumbling, fingers counting days: "Well, there's that fummin' fence line to

92

put up, poles t'come out, holes to dig 'n' that thingummy. Say 'bout three weeks' work on this contract in all. Be back 'ere ready with yer swag by four tomorrow, or I'll come 'n' pick yer up if you like. Well, that's that then. You got a job, see you later."

Mindfully slamming the door, jubilant down the street, Susan walked on sunshine.

Tanked up from an afternoon's bout at The Boab, Davie stumbled to the bungalow to sink in a gluttony of grog. Soaking back can after can until the early hours in the prosaic kitchen, simply lit by a central bulb; slothful torso supported by the blank white wall; speech fuzzy, abstract, punctuated with nauseously beery belches. Susan learned about his family and extended family and the cattlemen he had been working with, and their families and more cattlemen. Davie showed her photographs of when he was a boy at Mistake Creek. He was all smiles and affirmations.

"We owned all of this once, my family." Davie said he'd always look after Susan while she was in Australia; if she ever needed anything. "You're one of us now, see. If you ever need a place to camp, stay, y'know." And he undid her braid, pulling strands free. "It's so long," marvelled Davie. Then he tried to hold her down. She lost a silver ear-ring on the floor, they spent more time searching for the ear-ring than anything else.

"I need a woman 'ere, see. My woman no good." The stockman pleaded desperately, all those unspoken words begged her to stay. "You'll be right wiv me. I won't 'urt you." He paused. "Don't want sex 'n' all that stuff. Safe wiv me, you know that anyway. I'll look after you, like before."

Harrowed eyes leered bloodshot at a revolving room; ears tuned to Christine's belated outcry: "You pissed as a newt, Davie, leave the girl alone." Legless socked feet floppy on bruised linoleum, Davie reached his summit, guzzled the remaining dregs

93

and tippled over, dead to the world. Had there been a table in that austere cubicle, acrid with the odorous pickle of his caustic boots, Davie would have been under it.

It was regrettable that Susan hadn't accepted Callum's offer of a lift; walking the length of Derby with everything she thought she needed for a three-week camp, rolled in a sleeping bag, rolled in a swag, was a feat. Callum's yellow pick-up, TOYOTA filling the rear plate in firm black capitals, pervaded the drive. The back of the vehicle was piled with a mountain of swags, a fridge bedded on tools, a pneumatic drill, an enormous eski, white sacks of woven plastic bulbous with onions, tomatoes and potatoes, capping brown cardboard cartons and partially obscuring the word EMU, boldly stamped on the cardboard in red.

Callum's profile, minus one black hat, beavered over the pick-up's side flap as he strained to lodge a crowbar into place. A yelping red heeler darted out from beneath the truck at Susan's approach.

"Hi. Hey, Bushwhacker," Callum demanded, "come 'ere." Bushwhacker scurried under the vehicle, avidly beating its underside with his tail. "He all right. Won't hurt you." Callum's russet skin complemented the blue denims. He levered the crowbar down until it clunked. "See you got yer things. You ready? Yup? Chuck your swag on, we'll go pick up Davie." Susan burrowed her swag in the pile on the back and got into the front of the truck. Callum clicked his fingers. "'Ere, Bushwhacker, up, up." The dog obediently launched, scrabbling on a canvas roll, forelegs a-tremble.

Callum drove to Davie's without conversing. He hooted the horn, kept the engine running and hollered from the window. "Davie!" Beep be-ee-ee-pp. "Oy, Davie boy, ya bastard." One of Callum's traits was to use insults as a term of endearment. He

gave the horn one final lengthy blast. "Davie, you comin' or not?"
Out of sorts, Davie tumbled down the steps, into the truck and on
to the seat, shoving Susan against the handbrake. The door
slammed but was not shut.

"What, she comin'?" Davie said in fake surprise, releasing an
offensively stale cloud of alcohol.

"Yup, she's a'comin'."

"'Ard work fencin'."

Callum took off with a cavalier jolt, neatly reversed the truck
and curbed the speed as he glanced with misgivings at the
unstable load.

"You in a hurry," managed Davie, still inebriated from the
previous night's bender, binge clinging to his persona, secondary
smoke pathogenic. "Got me swag in?"

"Sure. Gotta pick up this other bloke yet an' tie that load down,
be bouncin' all over the road else 'n' we'll 'ave nothin' left when
we get there."

"Best tie that lot down or we'll 'ave nothin' *if* we get there."

Callum swished round the roads like he knew them with his
eyes closed, but he was a careful driver, checking in both directions before pulling out at junctions. He waved cheerily at just
about everyone he saw and pulled up outside a driveway a
semblance to his own, hooting vehemently.

A tall, wiry white man with greasy shoulder-length hair, an
unbecoming walrus moustache and the gawky features of a
scarecrow leapt after the swag he hauled over the fence. Callum,
already out of the truck, rearranged luggage. Davie and Susan
listened to them tie down the goods, and lurched on top of each
other as Callum rocked the truck, testing for secureness. Davie
hogged his former position, Callum was in again, and they were
off.

"Tight squeeze in 'ere," honked polluted Davie, wriggling to
exemplify the point. His eyes, fraught with lines, looked unusually
small, his groggy breath fermented. "Where's that guy then?"

"Stacked up in the back with Bushwhacker."

"Not much room 'ere." By now Davie was virtually taking up the entire seat. Susan, squashed on to the handbrake, hard between Davie and Callum's seat, offered to go in the back.

"You're right," assured Callum. "Davie, what's up? Give the girl some room, ya bastard."

Davie muttered, "I don't know," shaking his head, belching in disapproval. Then, like a drake in a dust-bath, waggled more space for his bottom. "'E a good dog, Bushwhacker, you done well wiv 'im since you got 'im as a pup."

"Well, 'e's all right. Not much of a huntin' dog though, real scared o' them goanna."

"What's that fella's name, one in the back?" asked Davie, signifying with his head, thus contorting Susan further.

"What or White or summin', not too sure." Callum cranked his head out of the window and shouted over his shoulder against the engine noise. "Hey, what's yer name? … Again? … What? … What?" The vehicle zigzagged, Davie corrected the wheel – cuffing Susan reminded him of her presence. "Can't 'ear, mate … What? … White? … White? … Wyatt!" Callum brought his head inside. "Wyatt. Wyatt. Says it's Wyatt or summin'."

"What?" said Davie in disbelief. "White?"

"*No*, Davie, Wyatt." To avoid the rigmarole being reiterated inside the truck, Callum spelt it out. "W-Y-A-T-T." Chanting, "Wy-att. Wy-att. Wy-att."

"That's a bleedin' stupid name. Got any beers?"

"Yes, Davie," Callum confirmed, drawing one, two, cans of Emu from behind his seat.

"She not having one," said Davie, grumpily pulling can tops, abstinence not being his method of recovery. "Can buy 'er own."

Callum asked, "You want one?" Susan didn't. "Shees, Davie, what's up with you?" No answer. "Grab me hat will you, s'behind the seat." Callum retrieved the black hat from his mate who had all but squished the last breath out of Susan, and put it on. "Your door shut?" It was rattling.

"Hm? What, me?" clowned Davie, opening the door liberally, nearly toppling out. He slammed it fiercely with a fright, grog slopping wonderfully.

"Ooohooh. Nearly killed me. Bleedin' 1990s and the bleedin' door won't shut. Ay, move over." The brazen-faced stockman boorishly attempted to make more room for himself.

"What she gonna be doin' anyway, cookin'? You gonna get 'er to do the cookin'? Says she can't cook bush tucker – well, she can't. I 'ad to feed 'er at High Rocky, didn' I. 'Ad to cook fer 'er an' everythin'. Coor, what you take her on for anyway?" Susan assumed these attacks were some kind of penalty or pay off for Davie's friendship. "Saw Owen earlier," he continued. "'E bin lookin' fer you."

"For me, Davie? What for?"

"Wanted to come out fencin'. I can't work with that girl."

"Won't 'ave to, Davie, she'll be 'elpin' me, diggin' them 'oles."

"She don't know 'ow, be better off wiv Owen – bin doin' it all 'is life. 'E knows this country an' all. 'E's family, Owen." Davie spitefully elbowed Susan. "Sophie, she all right 'bout the girl comin'?"

"Yeah, she's all right, still throwing them pots 'n' pans 'n' things." Undeterred by Davie's jibes, Callum was as elated as an adolescent faced with the prospect of driving friends out for the first time, delightfully flushed, energy flowing with every word, each sentence jestfully punctuated with "Davie". "Hey, Davie, 'member them days when we used to round up them cattle at Sun Creek?"

"Good days them were. Judith still there?"

"Jude's still there, she's there all right, Davie." Callum turned off the highway to the Gibb River road, sunshine showered in dust rained through the window and a cheery, beery atmosphere infiltrated the truck.

"Hey, Davie, roll me a smoke, mate. Tobacco's in the glove box, Davie." Davie opened the glove box, rummaging inside, his fingers found the flat tin of Log Cabin. "Papers're inside, Davie." Callum became abstractly amused at his friend's condition, which changed as dramatically as nature's seasons. "Davie, what's up, mate? Bin on the piss?"

"Feelin' crook that's all. 'Ad enough o' bein' in town."

"'Ad a gutful last night, eh, Davie?" Callum threw back his head in peals of incandescent mirth. "What's the use o' gettin' sober, hey, Davie, when yous gonna get drunk again?" Flying past scrub, gum trees, hitting the red gravel track with a bump as tarmac ended: it was wide country and open skies from now on.

Susan felt ridiculous being all cooped up with the great expanse outside. Davie rubbed against her as he kneaded a ball of tobacco between the palms of his hands, before shakily enveloping it in a paper. His impertinence dwindled after some hours of abstinence from alcohol (which had not come easy) and more slugs of the bitter brew. "You'll be right with Judie," said Davie with nostalgic honesty, "she'll 'ave jobs you can do. You'll 'elp 'er out." Davie retracted some of the pressure, Susan was happy, pinned between two pals. "She'll like Judith. She a good woman." Davie brightened up more as the grog went down, but in such a cramped cordon there really wasn't room for his gesticulations.

In the west the sun blazed on open spinifex plains and amber termite hills, which resembled obtuse cones of dribbled clay slurry. The cattlemen talked of when they were boys chasing raging rouge bullocks that could never be ridden, or riding after monstrously wild boars in a bull-buggy; told tales of gallant bushmen and of old droving routes. The pick-up hit a rock in the road, Callum reached his hand outside to readjust the wing mirror, his hat scuffed the side of the window, he cursed horribly.

"It's great to have a good yarn, eh Davie? We known each other long time now, Davie 'n' me. Best of mates."

"Best mates."

Callum turned right to Windjana Gorge. "Hey, Davie, 'member when we was feedin' in the moonlight wiv them cattle?"

"An' we couldn't find that blue dog?"

"An' we hadn't had smoko, or cut lunch, or nothin', workin' all day 'n' all night like that."

"'N' sleepin' in the saddle." The systematic, metallic click of opening cans, then the tales continued: tales of long, hot days in the cattle yard, of galloping from freak summer storms, Callum's first rodeo astride buck-jumpers in Fitzroy, tales of women and drinking and fighting.

Leafed with a hint of gold, the red rocks of the Napier Range rose ahead. Davie was his old self again. He smiled at Susan. "You bin to Windjana Gorge?"

Callum: "You know 'bout the Windjana, totem for our clan, Aboriginal totem. You seen 'im?"

Davie: "We'll take you there, swimmin' in the gorge."

Callum: "Big crocs there. You betta watch out."

Davie: "We'll watch out for you."

Callum: "In Derby, one tourist gets eaten every year by them crocs."

"Yummmm." They grinned at each other, pleased, conspiratorial. Peace prevailed in warm rays. All smiling, all dressed in denim. Words bounced off Callum's tongue. "Ol' Pigeon lived in them hills. You heard o' him, Jandamarra, our hero, Pigeon? 'E was an Aboriginal cop for the police back in them ol' days. 'Elped the police catch them Aborigines, helped 'em round 'em up and they were chained together in a long string. Big heavy neck chains they used. Used to 'old 'em in that old hollow tree just outside Derby. Ol' boab tree there. Then Pigeon, 'e turned 'imself free, turned against the police. 'E escaped an' 'e used to live in them mountains 'n' 'e 'elped the Aborigines then 'e did, waged a war on the police. He hid in them hills an' they couldn't catch 'im for years 'n' years. They used to hunt 'im with guns 'n' pistols 'n' one day, eventually, after years 'n' years, they shot 'im an' he didn't die, crawled through them mountains, 'long the Leopold Range to Tunnel Creek, that's near Sun Creek, where we're headin'. We'll take you there, Tunnel Creek. We'll be workin' out that way. There's a tunnel there goes straight through them mountains, that's where 'e died. You can walk right through that tunnel. It's long 'n' dark, need a torch, 'n' at the far end, when you get there, the opening is the shape of a pigeon. Like a big pigeon in the sky. That's where ol' Pigeon died. You should see that, we'll take you there. 'E's one of our national heroes, Pigeon. Yeah."

"Yeah."

A glorious dusk began.

Callum: "Just up 'ere we'll stop, show 'er Lillimooloora, that ol' gaol where the police held them Aborigines."

"She should see 'em things, part of our hist'ry. We betta stop soon, I gotta 'ave a leak."

"'Ave to wait, Davie. Not far to that gaol." The slant of Callum's hat concealed an irresistible smile. "You can wait, can you, Davie?" giggling and gurgling, "'E had too much piss." He braked and switched off the engine. "Bush turkey there." Dark heads peeked above golden grasses.

"Got yer gun, Callum?"

"Ner, mate."

Later they stopped at the old gaol. Statuesque eucalyptus grew amidst crumbling ruins of grey stone in a deep carpet of yellow tufted grass. Wyatt wandered around smooth bleached trunks, their long leaves dripping from branches coloured copper-red in the orange evening glow. Starry bindi-eyes threaded the weave of Susan's jeans, spiking her ankles with their spurs. Callum and Davie, haloed in an ochreous mantle, bragged boisterously about Pigeon and the police, each adding new aspects, illustrating, embellishing, flirting with the story.

Callum shouted, "*Snake*!"

Davie jumped. "Where?" Wispy blades of golden grass shivered with him.

"I don't know." Callum creased over, slapping his thigh in risibility. "Snake country this, they all round 'ere probly in this long grass." This charade was to be ongoing – Callum would shout "Snake" with a sparkle for forgiveness in his nut-brown eyes, Davie would be first to jump like a jack-in-the-box and Callum would elfishly coil up, his elastic face ripping with mirth. Happened again and again, always ending with Davie swearing wickedly.

"We betta move on now. Gettin' kinda late."

Lurid crimson mountains shadowed the pleated track and far supine pastoral plains mellowed from gold to coral pink.

Callum slowed the vehicle. "Hey, Susan, see that big buck kangaroo there, wanyjirri, see 'em feedin'? Plenty feed there."

Mysterious solitary boab poised provocatively on jagged pinnacles of rock, their stout trunks pillars sprouting spindly, lattice branches; their sprigs – outstretched, like fingers in a child's drawing – brandished the occasional circular nut. Taut, gnarled, slate-grey bark lustrous, perfectly lit in the fast fading light; surreal as the sheen of theatrical production.

Callum: "That range was covered in sea long time ago in … Dreamtime you call it. Called 'im Kakaji, Goanna, that mountain, see 'im, Goanna there. Still feelin' crook, Davie?"

"No, I'm right."

"You sure?"

"Yeah, mate, I'm fine. See 'em dingo dog? Yellow one there."

Callum slowed. "Where, Davie?"

"Jus' jokin'. No, look, for real. Dingo, see 'em?"

"Ssshhh, Davie," he hushed, "you'll scare 'em." Callum stopped the yellow truck, and sure enough, darting in the dusky half-light, through clumps of flossy grass heads mushrooming pollen into surf, were three scrawny, saffron-coloured Egyptian-cat-like dogs.

Callum: "Mongrel dogs, them. Eat the calves. Best tell Vince."

Davie appeared to be as thrilled as Susan. "You seen dingo before?"

"No, never."

The mountain's livid crags dimmed, their backdrop of electric peach-pink waned violet, studded with sparkling stars and a vibrant pearl-white moon. Callum switched the headlights on. A chilling darkness crept into the sky. Warmed by Davie and a belief that his renewed loyalty knew no boundaries, Susan was snug.

"Lying back between the flaps of my saddle," Davie sang softly,

> "By the campfire and the sun has broken through,
> All around me is the bush land and the cattle ..."

"Hey, ya bastard," moaned Callum, "wait till tonight, can't you?" But Davie couldn't.

> "While the damper cooks, I'm takin' in the view.
> Down beside the water hole the birds're singin',
> In a gum tree lookin' old as Father Time,
> And the stockmen to the station yards are bringin'
> Bush bred cattle for the draft and in their prime."

Weary from the perpetual jolting of the rough track's corrugations, all were thankful when Callum pulled up at the first rusty gate to the station house. Davie got out of the vehicle, letting in a cold river of air. Illuminated by the Toyota's beam, the last large iron gate of the station had startlingly bright white bars strung with pig wire; an old wagon wheel, fixed in the centre, was painted to match the metal. Sun Creek welcomed them under a chandelier of stars.

CALLUM LED SUSAN through dense darkness, across a colourless lawn, past a long, low rectangular building looming to their left like a big black void, and towards the yellow glow of the station house windows.

"Careful of the dogs 'ere, Freezer 'n' Blackarse, they'll bite you bad given 'alf a chance. Best not walk up to the 'ouse alone till they get to know you."

A small flight of steps, splayed with light, led to the station house door. Callum swung the door back, a woman welcomed him with open arms. "Come in! Come in!" Bedazzled by contrasting tonality, Callum and Susan adjusted their eyes to another drab, shabby station house living room.

"Hey, Judith, good to see you." Callum gave Judith a warm hug, then introduced Susan. The woman pulled up a seat for them at a formica-topped table where the arrangement of playing cards signified the tail end of a game of patience.

"Vince, come 'ere, look who's 'ere!" exclaimed Judith. A middle-aged man with an enormous gut traipsed up steps to an open doorway on the far side of the room. His white hair had a tobacco tincture, his complexion was akin in shading to Carl Roberts', only more pin-pricked with the scars of drink.

"Hey, Callum, good t'see yer. We'd given up on yer. How yer doin'?"

"I'm right. Good to see you, good to be back." They were all exuberant with the joy of old friends reunited. Callum went to embrace the man. Vince shunned him, nicotine breath rasping from the depths of his chest.

"Oh, I'm too old for that, got no time fer all that. I'm not too bad, eh, Judith, just older, eh," chuffed Vince in a broad West Australian accent; his eyes shone with undeniable pleasure. Callum introduced Susan to Vince who scoured her up and down in detached disapproval then cast his look, less disagreeably, at mute figures moving on a colossal television set, its prominence disinheriting a minuscule table, its luminance strobing the darkest corner of the room. "Jude does the cookin' so what you brought the girl for, Callum?"

"Davie say she works good."

"Black Pom, eh. Yous from England? Never bin there m'self. 'Ow's Pommy land then?"

Susan said it was all right. Okay.

"Okay," chuckled Vince. "Don't get to see many black Poms. Davie said summin' 'bout a girl on the phone, she gonna work wiv you an' Davie? Where's Davie to anyway? Callum, what yer done wiv 'im?"

"'E's out unloading the pick-up wi' that other bloke I brought. I'd best 'elp 'em, be back later for a beer."

"So you brought some grog then – bring any fer me? Judie don't need much, she don't drink much these days."

"Yeah, I brought 'em. Hey, I s'posed to be workin' for you. You s'posed to be payin' me," said Callum playfully, "not th'other way round."

"So, you're gonna leave the Pommy 'ere?"

"Yeah, you stay here, Davie 'n' I'll be back."

Callum left the room. The station manager shifted to a sagging green settee backed against the adjacent wall. His shirt was undone at the bottom, it exposed a triangle of tightly stretched skin on his hair-specked belly. He tugged absentmindedly at the waist of his khaki shorts. "Well, 'ave a seat, girl. Make the girl at home, Judith." Vince hawked, dropping into cushions. The movement must have dislodged something poisonous; his cough was so raucous it could have brought visitations. "Where's me beer? Get me a can from the freezer," spluttered Vince as he settled. "You can get one for the girl while you're at it … an' turn off that bleedin' TV!"

Years of strain from the grinding toil of slovenly station living ingrained Vince: a crotchety caricature of disgruntlement. Initially, at best Susan found him vulgar, yet she respected him, gradually becoming immensely fond of his brutishly low manner, although while in his company she always remained guarded.

Callum burst back into the room, gregarious, high spirited and out of breath from fetching and carrying, eclipsing care-worn Davie.

"That's one bloody helluva load in that truck," blurted the first man.

"Davie!" Vince and Judith rejoiced in unison. Vince moved to stand, then thought better of it. Judith was up, her arms embracing Davie. Barking dogs bounded into the room.

Judith, instantaneously freed from Davie, shouted sternly to the heelers. "Freezer! Blackarse! Freezer! Blackarse!" The blue dogs cringed, Vince growled and snarled mild obscenities until their retreat. Then it was beers all round. Davie and Judith sat at either end of the table, Susan in between; Callum slightly apart on a chair by the kitchen door; Vince sinking into the settee as the ends of the cushions appeared to rise. Merrily they drank and talked and talked and drank. Judith stuck to Sprites. Clad in a navy pinafore, she had the buxom figure of a middle-aged Aboriginal woman who had led a good life; her crinkled lines, though few, revealed that she had seen a bit of it too. One could read that it was not long since she had been one of the roses of the Kimberley, still adored by the men. Lush lashes gilded her fetching brown eyes. Her eyes, a furtive fire, flashed molten white

105

at Vince when he flung insults her way. When the provocation became too sordid the heat augmented and her usually hoarse tones rose to a scandalous crescendo. It was then the intangible ghost of the chemistry between them emerged: Vince would leniently back down, admitting that perhaps his lot wasn't so bad now that the ringers were there for Judith to cook for and to keep her company, too: "What the 'ell, keep 'er quiet," he could continue his life uninterrupted.

"Any left-overs from the boys' stew?" Vince asked Judith, who queried, "You wanna feed or what?"

"Course they 'aven't eaten. Go get 'em some o' that stew. Thought you said you'd brought another with you, Callum? Where's this other fella to do the fencin'?"

"Yeah, Wyatt, white fella, says 'e doesn't want t' come over, left 'im 'n' Bushwhacker back at the bunk-house. 'E bin workin' up in the Northern Territory or summin'."

"What you say 'e called?"

"Wyatt."

"Well, that's a bloody stupid name if you ask me." But nobody had, so Vince grumbled at that. In fact, Vince grumbled at anything when there was remote justification, and often when there wasn't. "Nobody asks me nothin'."

Davie chimed in. "Stupid name that, Wyatt."

Judith cleared the table, her robust earthy-black hands graced with a handsome elegance, the thickly formed nails efficiently stacking cards on two slim, soft-backed crossword books. She got up, turned to transfer her immaculate pile to the empty chair, then busied herself in a tiny square of kitchen. Returning with a plastic torch, Judith demonstrated the flagrant spotlight in the doorway to verify visibility before leaving for the bunk-house kitchen.

Vince burped and burred as he prattled about the main station, Kimberley Plains, and her smaller sister, Sun Creek, saying that in their entirety they spanned nearly one million acres.

All the land had been clear of cattle for years after it was designated a tuberculosis area. Wyatt and himself would be the only whites at Sun Creek; Kimberley Plains, belonging to two Aboriginal brothers, was on the up. Callum asked how the new stock were and how many; Frank Murphy was the new head stockman, how was he making out; how many ringers were in the bunkhouse; were they working well; what was the work to be done tomorrow? Callum took assiduous heed of Vince's replies while Davie downed Emus in splendid oblivion.

Judith heaved an aluminium saucepan round the door, withdrawing to the kitchen to reheat the meal. When it was ready she provided cutlery and a plate laden with stew, a benison to Callum; she dished out Davie's and Susan's – a steak dripping in gravy, rich and lumpy with carrots and onion rings, slapping blue plastic plates on the table before them. Appeased, Judith observed Callum, doted briefly, then seated herself. As she rolled a cigarette the lashes offset her eyes. She looked up and inquired after Sophie.

Callum's current was intermittently dammed with mouthfuls of meat, he talked of his family at length, described the horses he had been buying and breaking and the contract work he'd been doing. His mother had always lived in Derby. Callum couldn't stand the town's hustle and formal schooling was a juvenile gaol to him, so he had spent the best part of his childhood on cattle stations with Vince and Judith, gaining his grades through the government mail. Vince had been as unsparing as the sun when yarding up cattle, and dollars short as seconds – just as taxing as the time schedules at the school Vince had also escaped; there were no telephones then, just the bush telegraph. As those memories surfaced, Callum's pep eked out the jocular and the boy in him emerged, larger then than ever. The breaker was really at home.

Vince's drunken slur grated, his unsightly stomach erupted, intruding as he spoke. "Davie, hey, you gonna be up to fencin' tomorrow? Won't catch me out there with you mob. That Pom looks ready to drop. Davie, Davie-boy."

Judith said, "Let 'im be, 'e's right, eh."

"What me?" agreed Davie. "I'm fine." But his can was empty. Judith shoved back her chair, trundled out to the freezer for another round, her motherly stance noticeably wilting as evening turned to night.

"Get us one while you're at it," croaked Vince after her. Callum's lips formed an engaging smile, he looked to the floor, scooped up his hat, taming rampant raven curls, cocked it down in preparation for departure.

The distance between the station house and the bunk-house seemed to grow as he and Susan walked. Dowdy overhead fluorescent strips – a lethal lido for dancing moths – were the only source of lighting in the concrete corridor dividing sleeping compartments, they weren't brilliant, and the last one wasn't working.

Davie toured the dull bunk-house with Susan stepping behind. There were fourteen bedrooms in two rows; Wyatt was in the room on the right, nearest the entrance; Callum's was on the same side in the middle; Susan's next door; Davie's opposite; packed like sardines, the ringers were in another.

In order for Callum, Davie or Susan to see anything in their bedrooms they had to leave the door wide open. A small chest of drawers veneered in chafed pine-patterned formica and a wooden wardrobe were their only furnishings.

At the far end of the corridor was an unlit wash area. Facing the showers were pitch dark toilets (which Susan decided was a good thing because although to their credit there was an abundance of toilet rolls, the lavatories smelt bubonic. A deep inhalation, a breath that could last for the duration of the visit, was recommendable before entering).

Since arriving, Davie had been petulant and coy. "You gonna be right 'ere, Susan? Good. I'm right."

"Goodnight, Davie."

108

"Goo'night," he declared, harbouring dejectedly in the entrance to his room.

Undoing the straps of her swag that doubled as a bedding-roll-cum-suitcase and unrolling the whole lot on the floor, Susan took inventory of her possessions: spare clothes went on top of the chest of drawers along with washing things and towel, cashmere shawl folded at head end of swag, torch under it, alarm clock on floor, candles … she had forgotten about them, beside alarm clock. Out of pocket Swiss Army penknife, tobacco tin, lighter, all together in a jumble. What else? "Goodnight, Davie," again. "Goo'night," again. Door shut. God, it's dark. Clothes off. Groping for swag … into sleeping bag. One canvas flap folded over sleeping bag, other flap on top. Horizontal. Eyes tight. Silence. Footsteps. Silence. Timid knock. Silence. Davie's timid knock. Silence. Silence. Door-open-enter-Davie-door-close. Peering eyes. Silence. Footsteps. *Crash*! Must be the corner of the chest of drawers molesting the intruder, or the other way round …

Whispers: "Davie. That you?"

"Thought you said come in."

"What d'you want?"

"You, thought you said t'come in."

"Can't you sleep?"

"No. Can you?"

"What."

"Sleep."

"Yes, I think so." Susan fished for her shirt, sitting up and forward to put it on.

"Who's that?"

"Where? Me, I'm getting up."

It was impossible to see anything. *Thud*! Davie and Susan collided.

"No, Davie, no."

Crash! Sounds like the chest of drawers. *Bang*! The door. Door-open-door-close. Room erased to black. Footsteps. Silence.

Silence-in-the-darkness. Susan stumbled across the room groping for the swag. "Where's my bloody swag?" Shirt off, she slid into the sleeping bag. Tired eyes shuttered envisaging portraits on floors: the blanket-smothered stockmen slumbering nearby, black bodies entwined; Rikki and Pete, faraway in Derby, confined to a lock-up. Curling her toes into the padded cotton of the bag, Susan caressed softness for comfort. Callum cursed Bushwhacker from the room next door; Susan consulted her pillow, for sleep was adjourned that night, that first night at Sun Creek.

Outside were night noises. Inside, the walls partitioning each bedroom refused to restrain the faintest breath. Along the corridor an indeterminate range of snores mingled with Davie's wanton snore-grunt. Bushwhacker suffered a succession of nightmares, audible from whines or a series of whimpers, regressing to puppyish yaps. Prowlers creeping past Callum's door, venturing blind to the inconvenient toilets, were confronted with the dog's fearsome throaty growl.

Above Susan's makeshift bed was a small window from which she could see a patch of stars brightly peeping from a square of framed night sky. Secure in the bosom of ancient mountains formed by fossils of deep dreams – the sweeping sea of time; a time known to those with timeless knowledge: a time unknown – she went star gazing. Cruising the curves of a canyon's crater, tracing coralline crevices, indefinitely, in and out of slumber, she went night gliding. Susan never noticed the first light of dawn until after it had arrived, judging by his crowing, she assumed the cockerel had. Callum must have too, he was always up in what seemed to be the dead of night.

Near the exterior front wall of the bunk-house, adjacent to the washrooms, a small fire burned, this heated a metal drum to provide warm water for the showers. Judith cooked for Frank Murphy and the ringers in the bunk-house kitchen. Callum, Davie, Wyatt and Susan fended for themselves. Their kitchen area, those first few days, was a desolate plot of grassland situated

110

behind the bunk-house. Parallel with the back of the building, Callum had resourcefully constructed a food preparation table. The rickety legs were milk cans; the top, a laminated wooden door, wobbled under pressure.

They cooked breakfast on a voluminous upside-down rusted oil drum placed over an open fire; this stove was another of Callum's ingenious inventions. Out of the drum's base he had hacked eye holes – one square, one circular – and a grinning crescent moon mouth. On this anonymous gloat he placed a stew pan, frying pan and billy.

Making good gain through the brisk morning air, Callum and Susan sought kindling while an appetising concoction of tinned sausages, potatoes and onions bubbled under the lid of the sturdy stew pan, emitting tempting wafts, tailing them across the plain. Bacon sizzled, toast had been turned over the square eye, and the billy was boiling by the time Wyatt and Davie assembled, immobile as gurus on the largest log or an upturned milk can. Callum's kitchen kit was complete with every culinary utensil he imagined necessary. Susan thought of him as a cordon bleu of campfire cookery and shadowed him while the earth warmed, offering assistance as tasks unfolded.

During breakfast Davie was in discord. He behaved like a simpleton, displayed loathing and contempt towards his environment; from Susan he kept his distance and he neither greeted nor acknowledged anyone. This time Callum let Davie be.

Wyatt spent unenviable hours sorting out a heap of straight reclaimed fence posts from a gigantic stack by the bunk-house. These piles they all reinforced by repeatedly ferrying equally enormous loads from the dump, a short drive away, near the cattle yards on the far side of the main station track.

On the first day Callum rounded Davie and Susan up and the three of them drove out alongside a fence line. A cement mixer, tools and wealth of rusty pickets clashed on metal strips in the back of the yellow pick-up, a generator on the trailer. After

111

negotiating a ramshackle bridge, the vehicle submitted in deep dunes. Callum cleared a space in the rear of the truck, released the tail plate, and they took turns shovelling sand. The mound rapidly outgrew the truck's sides; that satisfied Callum. He described Sun Creek as "real pretty country". It was.

Undulating yellow plains reamed, its realm, patterned with gum and airy-leafed eucalyptus, was embroidered with prim emerald bushes to the indigo hem of a ridge of mountains embossing the sheer blue enamel sky. Artless posts, uninterrupted by any obstacle, an incalculable black regiment of unnatural regularity, solemnly marched through yielding grasses. The parted plain was to be replenished with cattle, the fence marked one of Sun Creek's boundaries; their task was to extend the fencing high up the hillside to prevent livestock from roving over to graze the neighbouring levels by the Leopold Range. Callum motored alongside the preceding spine with fretful Davie trickling perspiration in the front, while Bushwhacker and Susan jiggled with the fence posts, sand and the rest of the gear in the back.

Callum drove until the fence tailed off at the toe of a rocky hillside, he and Davie then clambered on scabby slopes, setting to work measuring and scuffing the precise pitch for poles. Susan gave her best, scrabbling in scree after them on all fours, handing up tools, slipping in shingle spores, holding pickets steady as the cattlemen gouged the hard surface and rapped posts into place with a sledge hammer. When the ascent became too steep and granular, Davie dug a hole with the crowbar, and Callum woke the generator, rousing a twittering myriad of tiny brown birds, euphonious in their airborne angst. Callum and Davie worked their way back up the new line of posts, smiting each one with a dolly, clangs assonant in hot air until metal hit rock. They ladled sand into the mixer's bragging mouth, making cement for the erection of two sturdy posts from which to strain wire. Callum eased five strands from a cumbrous, compact barbed roll, knotted them to the end posts, clenching and wrenching them taut with a strainer. Susan threaded metal ties through holes in posts, looping and securing them to wire strands.

A dimpled dirt road, imprinted with animal tracks like old, dented pewter, multiplied their mileage, charting them to three similar locations for fixing fence extensions.

Davie spotted fresh hoof prints in the dirt. Callum slowed to investigate and a herd of brumby galloped wild across the mountainside, swirling a kerfuffle of dust, paralleling the pick-up exhaust's twirl as they journeyed. With flaming manes and flaring tails, it wasn't until Callum halted at the edge of the range that the brumby disappeared over the crest.

Perched on the tail plate of the pick-up, Susan saw the dirt road wind, leaving yellow grasses way behind. She was cooled, for the last stretch of the ride, by eucalyptus lines on either side, their silvered branches coroneting the track with a leafy patchwork, dappling boulders overgrown with lichens, gloaming mossy and mild at the back end of day.

The station manager and his wife, mumbling across the lawn, came to greet Callum's truck. Vince hailed Callum as the pick-up stopped. "Wyatt's best building that turkey, Callum, 'e can start tomorrow, out by Tunnel Creek."

Susan hopped over the truck's side. Callum leant out of the window. "I gotta find a place where we can camp out for a few nights. So's we don't 'ave t'keep drivin' back 'ere to sleep when we're puttin' up that new fence line."

Judith cashed in. "Out by that haunted tree's best place. Ol' burial ground. Snakes there, eh," she cackled, "big mob, an' ghosts. Whooo-whooo."

At the prospect of going anywhere eerie, Davie was promptly out of the truck. Susan looked hopefully at Callum.

"You wanna come?"

She did.

"Eh! Mind them ghostssss," persisted Judith, "whoooo-whooo-whhoooo."

With four big bed frames and Bushwhacker in the back of the pick-up, Callum and Susan left Judith's ghostly tattle. Instead of turning left at the mouldering bridge as he had earlier that day, he made a bee-line for the Leopold Range, passing Tunnel Creek, sticking to the main track for a good five miles before turning right at the marker – a bush festooned with toilet paper. It took a few wrong turnings and a further half-hour of dusty driving to reach the intended camp.

Modelled like a shallow soup bowl, the site lay between the semicircular sweep of a mountain's foot and a copse of aspiring boab; the taupe, parched earth was honeycombed with lunar cracks peppered with sand. A breeze touched the concave arena, amplified by the curved mountain wall – a phantom voice from the valley preening, purling silent leaves to murmur. Vast shadows crept down from chilled precipices while the moon matured in an eerie, grave, everlasting sky.

Palms perspiring, pulses a-flutter, their bodies weirdly intemperate, Callum and Susan hastily hoisted bed frames over the pick-up's side to rest them under a cold ceiling, the finest boab's reaching canopy.

Callum cried, "*Look out! Snake!*"

Susan leapt sideways. "Where?"

"Jus' jokin'. Fummin' snakes everywhere 'ere. Fuckin' spooky place this," he gibbered. "Come on, let's get the 'ell outa 'ere, soon be dark, don't wanna be stuck with all them ghosts an' snakes all night, not yet anyways."

From the glade they scarpered to the trustworthy pick-up, their fleeting sniggers echoing, an inflated oddity beneath the discerning mountain's eminence. Callum turned the vehicle back to the station, their trepidation evanescent in a languid whirl of reddened dust.

"Davie ain't gonna like that place one bit, eh. 'E's spooked most of the time, 'e is, but that place ... mmm hmm," remitted Callum, smirking and shaking his head in remorse. "I don't know 'bout ghosts an' that, but there's summin' r-e-a-l strange there 'n' that's fer sure. Davie ain't gonna like it, even gives me the jitters, y'know." At each gate Callum stopped for Susan to jump out, from the open window he would yell, "Watch out f'them snakes!" And she would start in fright while fighting to free hoops of wire from the posts that drew back a section of fence for him to manoeuvre through. Streaming sails of copper dust they set off in the sun's fading glow on living mountains, their contours symbolising eternal creation.

Lips chapped, dry throats sore from Log Cabin strands, this was the hour when light was most magical.

"Can you roll them Log Cabin?" the breaker might grunt. "Roll me one then." The Tally-Ho papers, red on white in the glove box, were stained orange from dirt. "You like Country 'n' Western music?"

Susan smiled a happy blush.

Callum came to a plump halt, turned round and knelt on the seat, jerking it forward to forage behind the back. He ditched the empty beer cans and hauled out a plastic cassette player, grease smeared with inky fingermarks and coloured baby-pink. Then he tunnelled for a tape.

Blowing frothy dust suds glittering gold as they swelled and foamed around Susan's face in sunlit shafts, he loaded the player. "Still workin' then?" Tweaked the volume and, flashing a rogue smile, handed it to the girl. "Dan Seals. An old one."

As he drove, Callum sang snatches with the songs, his fingers snapping or tapping time on the dashboard; he knew each one by heart.

"Everybody says she's not my kind,
… City kinda girl …
She loves the way I walk,
I love the way she talks …
Saw your picture on a poster, in a café back in Phoenix,

115

Guess you're still the sweetheart of the rodeo."

Along the Leopold Range rose scarred metamorphic cliffs engraved with slanted images of forefathers' faces, enhanced at dusk, incarcerated with age. On ledges, in nooks, bloated boab grew, resorbing moisture. Floating from the tiny machine in the pick-up, musing, welcoming a breeze, those melodies might have been made for the monumental grandeur of those mountains they coasted.

By nightfall Callum pulled up at Sun Creek station. Susan faded from view to the black shell of her room. Exhausted and soaked in a sweat of achievement, Davie and Callum sat down side by side on the floor of the bunk-house corridor. They thought aloud under the profane light of the fluorescent strips, their backs propped against the wall.

Davie's knuckles were inflamed with bloody gashes from the fence's barbs. He took pleasure in affectionately channelling erratic colonies of ants around obstacles of dry grasses and dead moths with a stalk of spinifex.

Callum's smile was imminent, his dog captured between his legs. He recuperated, and annoyed Bushwhacker as he unwound by dressing the red heeler in a tatty white shirt. Bushwhacker was glad for the attention, not the clothing: each time Callum had one front paw imprisoned in an armhole and set to work on the other one, enlivened Bushwhacker had exited the first paw. Callum simpered, ambidextrously putting both legs through at the same time, smiling at his success.

Worming from his master's arms, Bushwhacker suddenly scuttled helter-skelter, paws skedaddled sideways, from the bunk-house, down steps, trailing the shirt, scampering into darkness, across the lawn to the motor repair shed, followed by Davie, Callum and Susan.

The two station dogs, prowling the garden, had traced the scent of a dingo on heat, tracked the bitch to the dump and

116

coursed her into the shed, where she was cornered under a wooden work bench, in behind Judith's truck.

The dingo bitch was a decoy to lure the station dogs from the yard, thus enabling the dingo pack to steal in and devour calves. Vince had seized his rifle, Judith was briefed with a torch: they were on the premises and pulled the light cord when the others crowded the building amidst a riot of baying, snarling dogs. Susan shinned up the back of the truck, ready to mount the blue cab top to ensure a prime view of the kill.

Ferociously thirsty, full of zealous devilry, the snarling dogs encroached. Benches lining two of the walls shunted, spilled tools scattered with the squall of beasts below. Hurling back and forth in her asylum, the bitch, overwrought with the near, pitiable climax, lost co-ordination, blundering into walls, against wooden table legs, fiendish hounds in close pursuit. Once a blood-curdling yowl rose from beneath the benches; once she escaped, lightning fast in the direction of the cattle yards. Susan hurtled over the truck's tail plate, past bystanders dithering in the doorway and out with the dogs who overtook the dingo, curbing her back to the shed.

The wild dingo, by leaps and bounds, station dogs in furious tow, was now chasing Susan. Running like the wind, in a trice she leapt on to the truck as the dingo fled to a treacherous refuge.

When the dingo bitch was dead, Vince hauled out the revolting dogs, flumping the limp carcass down in the dimly lit doorway. Judith and Davie dispersed. Vince stowed ammunition in the barrel of his rifle, summoned Freezer and Blackarse, and urgently proceeded to the calves' pen. Subsiding in the impromptu manner that it had begun, the event precipitated a transitory hush.

In poor light, Susan stood at the entrance to the shed with an over-view of the dingo: life drained from the bitch's eyes, her tongue lolled rouge over a canine fang to the sandy soil, moistly imbued with blood. Susan squatted and touched, cautiously, the damp, foxy coat.

Watching compassionately over her shoulder, Callum spoke. "Y'might think I'm bein' soft 'bout them but what with plannin' their attacks 'n' that, they're special." Arcane in darkness, he crouched behind. His voice sounded unnaturally loud and sad. "The government used to give dollars f 'dingo scalps, folks'd go out shootin' 'em, near wiped 'em out here: kangaroo, goanna, bush turkey, all them animals we used to have. We lived off 'em, bush tucker, berries 'n' that. They shot us people when they arrived, them whites did, an' the ones they didn't shoot they put to work an' rounded 'em up on reserves. Brought their diseases with 'em, near wiped us out again 'n' built their houses 'n' cities all over our land, pushin' us into desert. Now we got the mines an' cattle an' they're takin', destroyin' what's left."

Bullets cleft the night, Vince shot another dingo. Callum paused. "Gotta reach for them stars." His eyes focused on the quietened dingo. "We all gotta be strong, real strong, we're the lucky ones, we're alive." Callum paused again, watching his dog emerge from long shadows on the lawn. "Them politicians think we gotta live their way, learn 'bout their sciences 'n' that, that's what they teach us, sentencin' us to schools, they don't care 'bout the dreaming, 'bout our ancestors shapin' this land, the mountains, the rivers, fillin' it with living things drawn from themselves, an' it's bein' wiped out, wipin' us out 'n' all our beliefs, we all goin' in different directions now. We all at each others' throats like animals, only worse 'cos we're killing the land so's we'll have nothin'." The dog harried nearer with his tail between his legs, and butted the carcass with his poaching nose. Callum reached his hand into the light, casually dragging the heeler backwards by the scruff of his neck. "Some o' them whites keep goin' on 'bout the 'Aboriginal problem', they don't see that the problem's with them, with the way they think an' the way they're treatin' us, so we end up 'avin' to find solutions for all the problems they're

118

givin' us." Callum's gentle ethos was acute, Susan could hear the heeler lick his master's skin as if fawning in sympathy. A strain of poetry ran through her head: "What passing bells for these ..." Ruinous rifts and feuds had been her only experience of Britain's black communities. Sadness swelled inside. With abasement of heart, Susan had some understanding.

"As I see it," continued Callum, "life's a bit like them windin' tracks, I never know what's round the corner so I jus' keep goin' an' wishin', keep hangin' on an' ridin' through an' dreamin' for the day this world'll stop killin'. Some of us're okay, some still live out in the land. Me 'n' Davie, we're in between, part Aussie, part Aborigine. Sometimes I don't know whether we got the best of both worlds or the worst. Guess, up to a point, life's what you make it. We still know 'bout before, still got our totems, corroborees, we still go walkabout, go bush. But I never seen any of the hand-outs we were s'posed to be gettin' an' we still ain't got our land."

Lupine laughter howled from the station house kitchen where Judith, Davie and Wyatt sat at the formica-topped table, recalling how Bushwhacker had joined the fur-flying rampage while partly dressed in his master's clothes. Extraneous in darkness, their round of hilarity made a farce of Callum's words.

He shuffled forward. "I want more than to survive, exist. Life's 'bout the freedom to take risks. I really wanna live. I'm like Davie, can't compromise everything." Callum's lips were close behind Susan, she could feel his breath on her ear. "An' you, you can spread your wings or you can stay here; people's people 'n' most'll treat you right. Davie, 'e blows hot an' cold. Me 'n' Davie, we're only human. But when them city fellas say they can't see why we don't jus' fit in, blend in wiv 'em, I wanna say to 'em, if home is where the heart is, it feels like my heart's bein' ripped out." Disembodied cackles erupted from the kitchen. Callum turned involuntarily, then moved into light.

Susan edged away from the dead dingo to face him. His

119

features revealed nothing of the bitterness from the tiredest of circumstances, his skin was harmonious honey.

Callum murmured, "Don't you want to escape from your world to another where you own nothin' an' nothin' owns you?" When he looked at Susan with his soft brown eyes, she would have gone anywhere with him. Callum stood, turned his back on the girl. He had left her with the rumour of a place she could feel free, for this he was glad. As he walked away, Susan watched his mundane figure relieved black against the brightness of the homestead, his shadow stretched behind far over the lawn, his dog by his heels.

For the next two weeks, while constructing new fence lines, Callum, Davie and Susan camped out at the burial ground, working from dawn to dusk, eating meat mainly: bullock, kangaroo, anything they could catch. Most days Callum shot bush turkey, having borrowed the station rifle, so that was lunch.

Relief came at sundown when they drove back to the glade, parking the pick-up and station buggy in a protective V, which opened around the bed frames, arranged in a row to copy the arc of the last line of trees. Nearest the mountain range was Davie's, then Susan's; Callum's asunder.

Callum prepared the evening meal under the arms of a burly boab that stood a little removed from the glade. The base of the trunk had staved in on one side, a rotten hole gaped wide, shaping a hard-wood fireplace framed by scaly, weather-beaten bark.

Crouching beside the wooden hearth, Callum shook ash from a charred wire grate and wedged the grate into the fireplace, half-way up the mouth. Before him a sun set red, possessing all around. A precious time, the golden hour, when colours intensified before waning with the light.

In a lilac T-shirt and wear-torn jeans, Susan sat, restful, on her bed nearby, swinging her legs under the frame. Her face was tanned burnt sienna in the flame-hued light, flecked in her almond-brown eyes; loose locks plaid with sunshine carelessly streamed to her shoulders.

Callum glanced round, his smile quicksilver. "You think this place is stupid, eh?"

"I love it." Susan laughed back, for she had never met anyone so adorable. "I have friends when I want, and country. Beautiful country. And the moon. Tonight there's a full moon." She had shone milky all day in an aqua-blue sky.

Mosquitoes gossiped in a veil over Callum's bent back. His jeans were greyish with cinders, his heart was warmed by the girl. His black felt hat had a slim band of vertical black and white stripes, retaining a fluffy-brown bush turkey feather. When Callum split kindling, the chequered shirt rumpled. He sprinkled dead leaves under the grate, heaped touchwood on top, striking a match to the pile. Susan sensed him smiling, every now and then as ribbons of smoke unfolded, weaving round the ruptured wood of the hearth.

Callum knelt, crossed his hands in front of his thighs and knowingly stared at the country. Stony ridges, hollows, hills all dyed with a rosy haze, deep and vibrant, wholly inviting, praising bushes, trees, each balmy stem of whispering grass painted with delicate reverence.

Looking across the floodlit plain Susan felt different, better about herself, more confident, more carefree, could lose and find herself in one. She raked long fingers through her hair and felt at ease with the man. He poked twigs into the fire with the transcendent qualities of a chancing child. Beguiled by sable curls, his hazel eyes, a translucent nuance to cinnamon skin guarding artful ways. A flicker nibbled at stringy grey paper-bark twisting and blackening in corkscrew coils. Callum tilted his head forward, Susan watched him watch.

Skittering flames lapped awry as he stoked more twigs on the

121

fire. "Know what, Susan?" He wiped his hands on his jeans, and stood upright.

"No, what?"

Callum minced as he walked to the bed next to Susan's, leaning his seat on the metal ledge of the frame. "Broken my feet, back, neck, collar-bone an' one hand ridin' broncos an' been speared by steers an' horned by cows." Susan looked at him in surprise, for his physique remained flawless. "Vince learned me to grease saddles, stow all the gear away, an' a big mob of us went bush when the rains came." Then Callum joked about Vince teaching him to ride before he could walk by strapping him to a donkey, and Susan laughed until her cheeks ached. She drew each leg up under her chin and embraced her knees. She pictured Callum as the entertainer, a pure light: upstaging companions, laughing, joking, sanguine with each encounter, and was lost for words in admiration.

Callum laid his eyes on Davie who ambled by himself in the glade thinking of Christine. He had liked her instantly, too instantly. She never called him at the station. Wishing he had brought his guitar, Davie whistled to the cool evening air. From the topmost ridge of the range snaking round the camp were birds, diving down the precipitous drop, soaring up to scudding pink clouds, swooping to the branches hundreds of feet below. Trees took mortal forms, rooted to heartland; Davie, over-whelmed by the bulging trunks, shied, for each way he went he faced shadows that were gradually gaining ground.

The scenery was spellbinding to the girl and although Davie's friendship fluctuated, it still felt good to be near him. Crosswinds from the spinifex plain lightly touched her cheek. She looked up. The flitting black specks on the mountain wall caught her eye; green parrots, splashed with sunlight, winged their way through ruby rays, fluttering into sunshine, radiantly golden, the elixir of life.

Callum called, "Hey, Davie, what you doin'?"

122

"Who, me?" Davie jested, walking back from the glade.

Susan's skin flared amber and Davie sat up on the bed beside her, recounting the qualities of his infamous family, the Hobsons of Mistake Creek. Contrasting with his straw-coloured hair, his rare blue eyes gained an obliging blissfulness, his ruddy face blushed damson, and his coldness melted completely.

Susan listened in silence as she visualised hundreds of stock workers; from what Davie said, they all seemed to live on cattle stations and always had.

Callum felt sentimental about the past, occasionally chipping in with tales about his father carting wool around in a wagon.

"We should take the girl fishing, eh?" Callum might absent-mindedly say, remembering his childhood again: he was in the waist-deep water of a Fitzroy channel, no rod, just hook and line and the feel of flipping fins, the slimy, watery fish smell, pinky soft gills, ragged from his hook; their dry shrivelled shapes that earned him a boiled lolly from Judith's blue and white tin.

"Teach the girl to track animals, eh?" Davie laughed. At this Susan was really pleased. "After we've finished this fencin' work we'll take 'er, go bush an' teach 'er 'ow to track 'em down."

Callum returned to check the fire. "Yeah, mate," he said, thankfully settling steaks for grilling. "I've got me wife to think about, an' kids."

Davie had by now forgotten about Christine.

"Do you think I'm any good at fencing?" asked Susan.

Callum's sight didn't stray from the cooking; he flicked sizzling steaks over with a finger and fork, tiny bubbles of yellowish lardy fat popped and spattered. "Yeah," he mumbled, "you're doin' okay, why?"

"You would say if I wasn't, wouldn't you?"

"Aw, make yer walk back t'town." Callum jumped back from the grate. "This fire's bleedin' hot. Why, you wanna make a career out of it?" He smiled, inspiration beaming with earthshine humour.

123

"I don't think so," Susan said flippantly. "It's probably the most demanding, unimaginative and frustrating work I'll ever do."

"Hey, girl," Davie snickered in return, "I never seen anyone run so fast as you wi' that dingo bitch behind you." And they laughed at her absurd, astonished fright at that unforeseen contingency. The laugher echoing in the mountain wall laughed back.

Susan slid from the bed to stroll by the purply-brown bushes of the glade where dust merged with white sand from which rose thick, low shrubs, specked with colour. When she scanned the scrub with an overview, not focusing on anything in particular, the impression was dull, uniform, like a tattered woollen blanket. If she fixed her eyes on one point a vivid medley of hues emerged: tiny orange flowers boasting; snowy patches of cotton grass; brambly bushes; oval leaves; a harvest of variety. So much to see! Pink and blue buds, yellow blossom … but for the endlessness, they resembled the moors of the New Forest, reminding Susan of her childhood: the lovely smell of summer rain amongst flowering heather and gorse surrounded by yellow and red flora … freckles in the grass, she called eggs and bacon.

Colours fade with the light as it dies, and all at once Susan felt unwell, and rather out of place. Davie and Callum had their beliefs and hers conflicted with theirs – no, worse, she thought, her culture was destroying theirs, which seemed far more beautiful. She felt deceived by the cage of schooling, saw it as a prison of lies dampening senses and expression, yet knew her incapacity to escape all that had adopted her, the straight lines of education that ruled the pages of her life.

The twilight star was already lit. Longing to be rid of these confines, Susan looked up and into an indigo sky and wished from her soul that she could shed Western layers, the superficial values of a 'free society'. She imagined being a serpent flaying a stale skin. Susan loathed her world. Everything English was vile: bogus politicians in corrupt governments; the unfairness of democracy; the pomp, the gimmick, the squanderous manner of the monarchy; media hype; the discipline of armies, the anarchy of war; Christianity's greedy ego – mindless masses that renege; the hypocrisy of developing the 'Third World' (perpetually destabilising her roots, she thought indignantly). Genocide was inherent within all this philosophy. Anything to do with science seemed deplorable, dependent upon inane obsessions with lifeless possessions – the trivial dross ritualistically acquired swamping an over-populated planet enslaved by technological growth; maximising financial profits for a monopolistic minority who swish through life in sterile cubicles. All this she despised, all this she would shed – although it was all within her: Susan felt torn apart, and so much in the heart that she would never be happy if she returned to it. Most of all she longed to stay in the Kimberley.

Darkness fell, the shrubs in the glade sheltering the campsite could have passed for bushes of gorse and ling.

Before the evening meal they took turns to wash by torchlight in a plastic bowl. Davie knelt close by when Susan kicked off boots, peeled socks from her feet, stepped out of jeans and skinned off her T-shirt, draping these with under-clothes on the pick-up bonnet; water trickled down curves of old gold in darkness as she skinny-dipped in the bowl. Wary of snakes, Davie rolled tobacco, eyes peeping blue-violet from behind the vehicles.

To keep the fridge functioning and supply electricity for an overhead night-light, Callum had brought a small generator. This puttered consistently, adding a contemporary air to the mountain's primeval black shapes.

Hitched to the finest boab's reaching bough was the baby-pink cassette player. From this sagging arm, bowed at the elbow, a bulb dangled like a perky, overgrown fairy-light, forgotten, or abandoned after Christmas. Its fat black cable laced the boab's branches, its mantle hosted an active, attentive audience of feathery moths and made the velvet night seem even darker.

Nestling from the cold in her swag, wrapped in a soft hue of pendant lamp in trees, Susan loved listening to the Slim Dusty and Dan Seals songs commingle with the tempered warble of men's voices. Her concentration wavered through a mélange of syrupy soul-songsters' ballads, masculine dialogue, the timeless time, time present, times to come rippling into one, one within that primeval setting of the Kimberley. Here there were no relics, the cathedrals were eternally open.

Periodically the generator would stutter, the light flutter, talk idle and the tape lose speed. When the power packed up altogether the cicadas' chirp, commencing in unexplained unison, replaced slurred music, stringing a staccato serenade to the sleepy blade of crescent moon, arisen, creamy-white from the smug mountain tops.

Unsoiled by impurities, a tapestry of stars sparkled, parodying the synthetic lights seen of a distant town – those spurious glittering prizes winking goodnight. A warm wheaty odour rose from the earth, blending with the smell of tarpaulin, the seeds of Susan's dream.

When dawn lightened the sky they set off along the dirt road to start digging holes for fence strainers on Sun Creek's great plains. At this time of year most of the creeks had run dry. Gum and eucalyptus barred their banks, their grey-green leaves patterned with red filaments and silver. The pick-up dipped down a blanched sand bank; Davie and Susan, listing in the back, clutched the grooved sides of the vehicle as it shelved the fall. The notched boulders and roughcast pebbles of the creek bed stretched either way like a half-laid highway, making a choppy crossing.

Lying in the creek's reefy motifs was a king brown. The tawny snake must have been a good four foot in length. As the truck bobbed slowly over the creek bottom, wily coils uncurled; unrav-

126

elling sinister scales the snake lashed at the truck, skating the tail plate. Susan was transfixed in horror. Callum saw the snake's ricochet in the lopsided wing mirror, panicked, skidding to a halt.

"Fuckin' keep going!" screamed Davie. Callum slammed his foot full down on the accelerator pedal. The truck shot forward as the snake fluently recoiled, scaling and jiving in its camouflage.

Davie engulfed the girl in stocky arms, strapping her to his wet barrel of a chest; he all but lifted her up against his huge frame. She clenched her eyes tight; the warmth from his body subdued her fears for the rest of the journey.

The first site, encircled with gum and eucalyptus, was set back from the road. Callum unloaded tools amidst termite hills, rising red from yellow grasses, shimmering in a mirage to the horizon's blue.

"All you have to do is keep hold of this bar," instructed Callum, welding Susan's fingers round the warm bent tube of metal forming a triangle below the drill's motor head. He stood behind, gloved her hands in his and, converging their bodies, pushed forward, clapping Susan's stomach against the bar.

"Just keep hold real tight an' press down, I'll be on the other side keepin' 'er steady. Jus' try an' keep pushin' down an' away from the direction this blade goes in." Callum drew a spiral in the air. "That way she'll keep goin' straight. Be r-e-a-l careful, she hits rock, she stops dead, an' that can be a shock."

"You think she can hold it?" a concerned Davie asked Callum.

"She'll be right." The lesson progressed. "If the drill stops, if she hits rock, you jus' let go 'cos she'll buck all over the place an' you'll get hurt bad an' the drill'll prob'ly break 'cos she can't cut through rock." Callum lowered his tone in earnest. "You think you gonna be right?"

"I'll do my best," said Susan, who had no idea what was required of her.

"Okay, when you see me nod it means the hole's deep enough,

but I can't turn the drill off till she's clear from the ground otherwise she won't come outa the 'ole, right?"

Davie smiled blithely. "Why not let me show 'er first?"

"Nah, she'll be right."

Callum stepped round Susan and clamped hold of the symmetrical bar on the opposite side of the drill. Ham-handed, he and Susan lifted the cumbersome machine and wavered, teetering over a lean cavity they had gouged in the earth, lowering the blade tip to station it in the centre of the graze.

"Ready?" To start the drill Callum energetically tugged the retractable cord interminable times; sweat droplets bedewed his face and jewelled his lashes, his eyes were fixed on the girl's. "Fummin' bitch won't start." Callum's words were swamped in the engine's earth-shattering roar, and they were jolted into action.

Violent pneumatic juddering permeated their bodies, causing their faces to flicker with palpitations; the amount of effort required to force the drill upright came as a shock, vibrations left hands numb. Using their entire weight, leaning left, waging their might, straining every muscle against stubborn jerks, they slogged over the thrust of the drill's cradle. Susan, shaken to a flush, caught Callum's candid gaze. He mouthed a word but it didn't resemble "stop"; she felt certain that if they didn't stop soon she would fall apart.

Juxtaposed against the violence of the drill, Callum's mahogany hair, skin bronzed auburn, terse lips perfected, were a tonic; his steadfast stare, the sky. Clinging to scalding metal with throbbing heads, crooked backs and legs quivering. Diesel fumes vomited, the sun breathed down. They dug so deep that their chins shaved the bar. Then Callum lifted his gaze to the sky: it was his nod to start levering the blade up. Both rivalled to unplug the drill from the hole, carbon air sucked *whoosh* as the engine died and dirt sprayed from the blade's decelerating revolutions. She was free from the ground. Ardent and barren was the empty heat, silence sang in stunned ears.

"Lay 'er on the ground," gasped Callum, "over 'ere, on 'er side. Don't touch that damn blade, she's bloody hot." He and Susan lumbered, dehumanised, half dragging the machine's gruelling weight.

Quaking from the ordeal they set the mechanism to cool, even after they had put it to rest, Susan's fingertips tingled from the sensation of the tool. She found it macabrely erotic to invade the earth with an inflexible drill while working with those men. Callum was first to regain his countenance.

"Crowbar's in the pick-up." Susan fetched it and handed it to Callum. Reinserting the black pole between her hands he said, "Can dig the hole out so the sides're even."

The sides of the hole tapered to a cone, the base was hidden by shadow. Bone weary, Susan probed the yawning mouth, chiselled seams and pummelled bedrock. Callum wiped sweat from his brow and watched despairingly.

"Never used a crowbar, eh? 'Ere, lemme show you." The breaker's stalwart biceps bulged, Susan could taste the pungent smell of his sweat as he pounded the pole in the chasm: down-up, down-up, down-up, rhythmically slicing the sides.

When he handed the crowbar back Callum's glistening face was stippled again with beads of perspiration.

Prepossessed by feminine contours, Davie strutted around. "'Ard work this. Push 'im down 'ard. 'Ard work." Susan repeatedly attacked the depths of the hole, aping Callum's actions with minimal effect. "'Ere, gimme." Davie took the crowbar, continuing the beat; Callum, then Susan, until the cylindrical chasm's sides stretched smoothly in a vertical line.

Flat on his chest, Davie laid his shoulders over the mouth, reaching one arm down the length of the opening to scoop out subsided subsoil and stones with a tin until the touch of the base was at his fingers.

129

After that hole they dug two, three more. Susan's endurance swayed, the half-submerged blade kicked back and she was catapulted into the air.

Callum spontaneously whooped: "Yeeha!" Susan hit sward disoriented, prostrate, too afraid to move. "Hey now," Callum cooed, unease perturbing his composure, "musta hit rock 'n' locked or summin'. You right?"

Davie ogled over Susan's body, scratching his thatch of fair hair with one hand, the other muzzling his mouth. "Musta bleedin' killed the girl." The men waited. Droplets of Davie's sweat fell in Susan's hair. She wasn't hurt. She sat upright and to her dismay the sequence continued: four, five, six holes; digging with the drill, Callum's eyes invigilating, singed sand sousing carbon air, rock chipping with the crowbar, pruning, excavating fractured stones, flints; blisters burst, blistering again.

Davie poured porridgey cement into each hole, Callum set posts for a gateway, or yards apart as strainers squared with an eye-level. Where each post sprouted, splattered cement blobs blotted the sand.

At smoko the flies swarmed unabashed. Davie and Susan gathered eucalyptus leaves; Callum collected wood, dry, satin smooth and grey, gaily snapping the sticks as he went. Blue where hills met the horizon; a perfect mackerel sky on blue dyed the distant mauve hills. While waiting for the coals to smoulder, Callum covered the thawed meat with fresh foliage, arranged damper and twists of salt in silver foil. Davie boiled a billy and they sipped sweet black tea from their pannikins; in the bane of flies it was no picnic.

Davie, the chameleon, found honey in a tree; he stole the sweetness, sat on a log within reach of the fire, sharing it out from a sheet of silver foil.

"Purrula. Call 'em sugar bag, these bees," he said to Susan. Bawdy bees entered every unprotected orifice, humming and buzzing intolerably. By the time Davie had removed a blackened

130

rib bone from the fire and they had put it to their lips, seething flies and bees had already banded together, sucking juices. Each charred mouthful scrunched, battered in charcoaly layers of bees.

Davie was overcast with distress; he threw a half-chewed rib bone aside, jiggled and swiped at the insistent pests. "Don't sting, these bees, jus' bite an' drive you mad. 'Ow's a man s'posed to work?" In desperation he flung green branches on the fire, creating clouds of aromatic smoke. Davie cowled the coals; then Callum, then Susan came close. Demonstrating how much he cherished life, Callum's free spirit flaunted contagious joy, unleashing heady, free as air, laughter; for their bodies shook with bees and in a fit of heebie-jeebies at the monotony of insects, they were all hopping, yawping uncontrollably with honey on their lips. Astride the ashen branches, they could see nothing for smoke and streaming eyes.

Clouds on the horizon retreated after noon, revealing another mackerel sky for the sun to break through, and then a system for building the fence line was finally established. Davie, squatting in the back of the pick-up, passed black metal fence posts up from a heap to Susan, who threw them out over the tail plate. Dragging behind the vehicle was a fence post fastened at its top by a length of rope, the other end of which was tied to the tow bar. When the head of this post was level with the mark made by the last post she had cast, shouting the count Susan hurled another, spearing the ground immediately behind the exhaust, distributing them at an equal distance.

At fifty they stopped to scar the ground for a strainer to be set or, in accordance with Vince's scrawled map, two gateposts, and deposited bundles of barbed wire. In this fashion, with Callum driving at a snail's pace, throttle deliberately down, the yellow pick-up crawled in a straight line, a hair's breadth from a slack strand of wire laid on the ground for guidance.

Marble clouds regally edged with purple and mercury delivered the vanilla sun. Davie and Susan retraced the line on foot, ramming in posts as they went.

Callum waited at one end to align the posts by sight, hailing instructions. "She wants t'come to the left. No. No! That way, yeah. Jus' a bit more ... bit more ... too much. Yeah, better ... better. Okay. Left again. Right, next one." Davie and Susan worked their way back, all the way along the line until Callum was a blip, commands barely audible, and he scanned the bones of their workmanship, straight as an arrow, with easy appreciation.

They spooled out four parallel lines of barbed wire from rolls revolving on a rusted bar attached to the vehicle's chassis. Up high, set in blue, a moon tenuously watched the day, awaiting her turn, for it was her fate that, after her shining, she waited again. While the men tackled with the strainer, clinching lax strands rigid, Susan maundered her way down the starched line, methodically threading metal ties through eye-holes in each pole and hooking a strand of wire. During this tedious task, when all the strands were taut, and the pique of midday heat had sluiced over oceans of grasses, the tizzy of flies had flown, and it felt as though they were the only moving creatures left on earth.

The men laboured behind Susan in single file along their ostensibly victorious boundary, bowed heads bobbing like grazing ducks in a row as they stooped to pair stiff ties with posts and resistant lines of wire. Once the afternoon flies had come and gone again, the frustrations of the day were healed with the slow sinking of the sun, and one could never guess the simple satisfaction the sight of a completed fence line would bring.

One morning Davie and Callum drove a double-decked cattle truck from Sun Creek station to Leopold Downs. Susan was to follow the men in the weird open-top contraption Davie referred to as "the bug". Callum had left his dog with the girl and a generator, seated on the back of the trailer.

They called those two-deck trucks road trains because they were so long, dust streamed like smoke from a steam train. As Davie pulled the truck away, dirt clouded the wagons. He cleared his throat, sputtering at Susan through dust.

"Yous can stick behind, right?"

Coughing grit, the cattle truck clattered and clunked on a broken track. Susan drove behind until, concealed by a slip-stream of chalky smog, the cattle truck vanished. She drew the bug aside for the obscuring sediment to settle, was left behind, and lost.

Why is life so full of problems? Susan said to herself, getting out of the buggy. Bushwhacker whimpered, clambering from the passenger seat after her.

A tree stood alone on the prairie, black branches spliced the sun. A lizard slithered, sand slid, as windswept as the plain. Susan watched the sand, thinking of Davie, she just couldn't place her feelings for him. She did feel happy when they were together. The dog sniffed at the spiky ochre-brown grasses and looked at Susan with loving eyes. She grabbed one of his pointed ears, knelt down and gave him lots of fond pats; Bushwhacker shook his head and kept pretending to sneeze. Susan's thoughts stayed with Davie. He was like her. But there was a gap – now and again his assurances suddenly gave way, which was terribly disconcerting. Was it love? She wasn't sure.

Confused and unclear, she wandered along the fence line, the red heeler trotting quite happily after her.

Pink-eared bats are rare creatures. Susan found one dead, worsted in gossamer, trussed in the fence line that sunrise. Its surprised snout poked from a furry inky-brown body; its ears were enormous, flushed with light, blushing flaming pink, lucid veins all aglow.

When she returned to the buggy Susan decided to make metal

ties for the fence line. She started up the generator which, blowing heat, powered a circular blade with a serrated edge for cutting wire. Susan sat in the sand under a tree and fed rolls of wire to the blade. Spewing hot granules of metal, the blade sliced the wire, producing six-inch stems.

The sun burned Susan's shoulders. The trivial gum gave poor shade and thrived with bugs and ants which dropped irritatingly from its branches. Bushwhacker panted exhaustively and when panting became too hard, retreated under the trailer to stick, motionless, to shadow.

It was extremely hot. Susan began to feel intensely annoyed, faltering as she toiled. Davie should have told her about Christine. Why had he behaved like this? What did it mean? How did he work? Did he feel cheated in some way? She wanted to know, to know Davie through his world, and Callum was part of that world.

Thinking of Callum, Susan was comforted. She forced together the ends of each metal sliver, to form a U, as Callum had demonstrated, cropping the ties in the sand. Callum had predicted that the return journey would be no more than an hour. It felt like four.

When they found Susan, he pressed something small and hard into her hand. "A gift. Call 'em rain stones." It was an exquisitely beautiful gem, transparent, like clear quartz. Callum's eyes shone, his smile was a soft caress: to appear faultless was his forte. He reached in his pocket for a small cluster of the lucent minerals, and they marvelled at their perfection. Pondering in anticipation, Callum drove, and gleaned the ground for more. He stopped at a patch of red earth spangled with promises glinting ideally. Struck anew with nature's achievements, in charm they gazed.

Davie, eminently enchanted by the stones' beauty, plucked at the earth's surface. "Miracles!" he clamoured ecstatically, placing a dainty crystal on the flat of Susan's palm. "Like hail that never thaws."

134

Davie was up most nights, guzzling in the stew pot which was nearly, if not totally empty come sunrise.

"Oink! Pig's bin an' eaten our tucker in th'night," Callum would proclaim, "if only I could catch 'em." Davie preferred to remain silent, never admitting to the moonlit raids and midnight feasts. But the scrap-licked bowls and pans became such a regular occurrence that as the three fell asleep, Callum would lie in bed giggling and gurgling like the rascal he was. Susan remained neutral, Davie's reluctant excuse was that he'd never steal food, the glade was too spooky to wander round at night "what wiv all them snakes 'n' ghosts 'ere, I'm bleedin' petrified."

Davie's unprecedented snore was the most prominent noise, and enough to wake the dead. Once Susan saw him stricken with fright, hair on end, looking like he really had seen death alive.

Clutching cigarettes, they looked to their gloam in a black film of night, every bone moaning unwillingly. When dingoes howled Susan reached for Davie in darkness; an algid wind whipped her face – the stockman was a time away. He'd snort, or snuffle, while the wind's rustle tickled the tittering leaves.

Fire in the hollow of a boab's gnarled skin, svelte entrails of smoke, smoky-blue swerving, wheeling nymphs scowled through static branches' burbling leaves; stomachs squabbled, churning for food.

Callum was up, lusty and lively in the dim dawn, carefully packing the few remaining Emus, Stubbies and VBs into the largest eski as though they were fragile ornaments moving house.

To continue her apprenticeship Susan spent a day helping Callum solder in the shed at Sun Creek station. When he drove back to the camp he said they would be moving the next day, sleeping back at the bunk-house.

"An' the next day after, I gotta go back to town, sort out some more contracts, fill up with fuel 'n' pay for all that beer Davie's been drinkin'. See that white yute comin'?" Callum pointed to the approaching vehicle. "'S'Phillip Fingers, overall manager for

135

these stations, we call 'im Phillip Fingers 'imself. It's an old joke," said Callum, catching Susan's eye to see whether she had understood the innuendo. Susan felt uniquely privileged to be allowed in on one of the men's rude jokes.

The white yute's speed decreased, as they drew nearer, both drivers braked level. Phillip's fingers sported a cancan along the open window ledge while he and Callum talked. Susan eyed the fingers with such intrigue that she never saw Phillip's face.

Callum revved the pick-up's engine, drove through clearing dust, repeating the nickname with lavishly cocky benevolence. "Anyways, you can come back to town with me or stick 'round 'ere, Vince could do with a hand, I'm sure, an' you can 'elp Davie out with the fencin'."

Susan said she wished they could stay at the haunted site forever. Callum said, "Really?", beamed, and they laughed together because they loved Davie – aptly concurring that this was the best life there is.

There were rock pools near the burial site where they could bathe. Before leaving the camp they drove far deeper into the bush than they had ever been, in search of them. Dawn sunlight stroked the mountain tops, the sky was fantastically clear.

When the steady incline and dense vegetation became too much for the buggy, they picked their way through thickets of clawing undergrowth, enmeshed with twining creepers' tendrils strung with clinging spiders; past bushes abundant with berries and nuts, decked with floral garlands, brushing aside springy stranded canes, low thorny boughs lashed back. Crisp leaves, undisturbed since falling, shuffled and crunched under munching feet, new-born shoots of fresh lush grasses peeped verdant needles, succulent ferns stroked ankles. Bare feet clambering, climbing crooked crags, a foothold pointed out, a hand-up for leverage. Without speech they rose up the galvanised gradient, the sickle-shape sweep of the mountain range sheltering the remnants of the camp. Far above the hum of cicadas, over grey granite boulders – queerly balanced, warmly alive, smooth to the eye, rough to touch; streaked with ochre, frothy glaucous lichens, rusty-red iron deposit and black scars. The cliff grew more finely defined, features jagged, steeper. Absorbed in the wild perfection of the earth's crust, senses heightened, in turn they lost their footing. Davie grabbed the back of Susan's collar, hauling her up the slab's sides – pulsing with vitality, power from the sun. For these were the omnipotent faces of the past whose divine sovereignty glowed fiery crimson-mauve as heaven closed her eye. Sky high, saddle obscured from sight by boulders, the precipice diminished to a head of rock, rounding off to form a bald burnished brow.

Here the ore lay in curved terraces whose ironed velours were muddy-brown; the air was clear, joyous birdsong piping all around. On this table land, sunk in metamorphic slabs, were black water pools on different levels, ominously deep, dark pools, some adjoining each other, some separate, increasing in size as they continued on a crease in rock – a polished path winding on precious stone.

Before the terrain tapered sharply to the range's rugged summit, they reached a plateau of little oval lakes. An oasis; a sacred place. It felt strange and wonderful. They cat-walked the perimeter of the largest pool. Callum's rash drawl broke their awed silence.

"There's a rock python that's fourteen foot long livin' at the bottom of that pool, strangles people." Susan peered, seeing nothing but glassy reflections sustained in still blackness. Higher up she saw a cavern, tall enough to stand up in, littered with twigs and dry leaves. She had wanted to enter until Callum said it was the snake's lair.

"We'll wash 'ere where it's flatter an' them big pools're deeper, you go further down the mountain. You be best at that first pool, down a bit."

Stealthily she retraced the chamfer paving the way to the lowest platform, undressed, dropping clothes carelessly, to sit on the smooth recess that formed a shallow step at the edge of the first black pool. Consumed by the environment's enigmatic equilibrium, naked. Alone.

Susan wondered how many serpents squirmed beneath the formidable glassy surface and how the men could possibly sum up the courage to break the calm cover. Faint and soothing, the sounds of men splashing and bathing above, unaware of her dread, floated down, washing a wave of humility for feeling impiety in such a sanctuary.

She stared, hands clenched on rock, allowing a rigid toe to be swallowed, a foot, teeth gritted, two feet reaching for, timidly feeling, touching a seemingly bottomless bottom. Lowering her whole body, wide-eyed and trembling and so thin from fatigue, into the mute, menacing darkness of intimidating black water, the finger of fear creeping up her spine. Unbelievably submerged, every split second imagining snakes coiling, writhing, strangling in darkness; yet despite the fear it felt gloriously refreshing, sinking into silence, to disappear from an unclear world to cooler, murkier depths. The sun warmed her shoulders. Seduced by the soporific, leisurely muffled voices reverberating down the mountainside, Susan, immersed up to her neck in her black water pool, basked and soaked.

Coolly, cleanly, a dewy band of three emerged: the men's hair slicked back, compact with sequins dripping; skin radiant from days in the bush; revitalised, scrambling from mysterious heights.

The blades of a windmill, oblique and severe, revolved against a vast opaque mounting, otherwise uninterrupted. A grey smudge of ashes lay under the water tank. The dank washrooms, smelling of cockroaches and sickly cheap soap, each with their insipid trickle called "shower" said, "Don't think, just feel the silence until the soft pull of the first can opening."

In the gloomy corridor Davie sang "No Campin' On Old Ivanhoe" and "Joe McGuire's Pub", chord strumming or skilfully string-picking his guitar. He yelled, "Watch out for 'em snakes," when Susan entered her room; she envisaged masses of slithering serpents violating the floor. Callum asked Susan whether she would like anything from Derby. Susan settled for oranges.

"Fuckin' Pommy veggie grub," came Davie's genial reply. "Anyways, we'd be better off wiv Owen, 'member, I told you. Hey, Callum, you bring 'im back, eh?"

Vince sneered beerily. "You 'aven't run back to Pommy land, thought you'd've gone back to Pommy land by now." His tone left her feeling he wished she had.

Callum stole across the dismal corridor to fetch another beer from the deep fridge, Davie's husky, opportune call trapped him. "Hey, that you?"

"Yeah, you want one?"

"Bring me one then." The session continued.

Stars were the only brightness that night in their diminishing land; with bitter strands of tobacco on tongue, they used can after can for ashtray.

WHILE CALLUM was in Derby Susan slept a lot: sometimes her dreams were better than reality.

It wasn't often that a vehicle ventured through Sun Creek. If one was heard on the track Susan's ears pricked up, that it would be Callum seemed a certainty. A week passed, there was no news from him.

The far end of the range, noble, majestic, fiercely charged, domineered the scene while she pulled up fence posts for the first two days. Back and forth the buggy happily chugged, drenched in an amber-white hue – the euphoria from mountain ridges, vibrant at dawn or eventide.

Spooked by red-back spiders that haunt the grasslands, Susan moiled waist-high in grasses, tugging up rusted posts, many of which bent and were then useless, from cracked soil callous with drought. Scorched by a sun with no clouds to hide behind, these days were spent in solitude.

At night Judith said the place was full of spirits. The ambience was certainly analogous to the burial ground with its eerie presence. Vince was admirably impressed with Susan's efforts, harping on about the number of posts she had retrieved, and in such a short time. He even helped her unload the buggy to replenish the stack of used pickets in front of the bunk-house.

It was another turn of events that stirred Judith.

141

Susan had dropped Wyatt off at Tunnel Creek and was about five minutes into the return journey when the buggy's engine stammered, grinding to a halt under the arms of a sturdy boab. Fiddling with the key in the ignition had no effect. The extent of her mechanical knowledge drew her to the conclusion that the fault was electrical – something disconnected. Ferreting in the back amongst odd strips of oily rags, hessian sacks and filthy tools cluttering the floor, resulted in her discovery of a small, blue, hive-shaped eski and an eroding enamel cup. The eski contained a putrid dribble, barely enough to cover the cup's bottom. Susan removed the key from the ignition. There was only one way forward. Walk.

Prickly thickets, gum, eucalyptus, faraway mountains blue behind blue, distinguished the expansive sphere to the right of the track. The stolid face of the Leopold Range, imperviously supreme, reared left. This frigid façade's features, flattened at midday, brought back unwanted memories: effervescent Davie, sprinting from spirits in a crevice at the gulley of rocks; the king brown lashing at the pick-up; a puffy death adder flaccid, centimetres from her foot. In that tremendous country's stifling heat, the further Susan continued, the more overbearing the bush seemed.

Shadows shrank from the sun, shrubs shuddered in a non-existent breeze, eccentric noises she had never noticed before menaced from the bush. Quickening her pace, Susan didn't dare look back, it felt as though someone – something – was on her trail. A rumble from afar transformed into a dust-shrouded vehicle that shot by, blinkered to the roadside hitcher in its desiccating wake. Squalls of wind whisked willy-willies, whirlpools of copper-coloured dust, that flew down the track in precocious, miniature cyclones.

Susan reached the gate always sheltered from the sun, where obtuse boulders overhung and sapling boabs fattened at all levels of the cliff's heights. There was a sigh from the mountain's heart;

a land cruiser, heralded in dust, scudded the corner. Susan swung the gate back on its heavy hinges. The vehicle slowed; at the touch of a button the window slid, revealing a woman's lobster-red face.

"Excuse me," Susan said, "my truck broke down on the road back there, please would you give me a lift to the station?" The face contorted into the graphic expression befitting one who detects the whiff of a carcass decaying in heat. As soon as the plate of glass had hit half-way, it retracted; the air-conditioned land cruiser accelerated in searing dust. Yet to Susan all this seemed to happen in slow motion: the metallic body with smoke-tinted glass, the woman's morose face, the events in reverse, the dust.

"So 'ow d'you get back 'ere? D'you walk, eh? Like walkin', eh?" chuckled Judith when Susan reclined at the station house table.

Bringing the misadventure back to life, Susan explained what had transpired with the vehicles and how she had tried to get a lift, her tone raised as the tale unfolded. "Oh Judith, I had a terrible time, it was awful," she stressed, remembering her relief when the land cruiser had stopped, and then the woman's look of repulsion. "I had to walk, I had to walk the whole way. I thought I'd never make it but I did. Anyway, what I'm worried about now is Wyatt's stranded there at Tunnel Creek and the buggy's broken down so I can't pick him up."

"Leave 'im. Best place for 'im."

"*Leave* Wyatt at Tunnel Creek? I thought Vince might be able to come out."

"Vince is busy." The woman was cackling, high with her impetuous wit. "Get Frank, one o' them ringer mob. Y'show 'em where 'e's to later, eh." Judith retreated to the kitchen sink, rinsed her hands, drying them on a towel. "An' before you go you can catch that goanna. Catch that ol' one by the scrap 'eap, 'bout time 'e was got. Big one. You seen 'im?" Susan hadn't. "'E's one

143

mighty big tough ol' one. Catch 'im an' I'll cook 'im in the ground, 'e tastes a bit like tangy chooks. I'll make damper, we can eat 'im then. You 'ad goanna? Cook 'em in the ground. I'll show you."

Nodding feebly, Susan shunted her chair into the cool blow of an electric fan on the table; more comfortable in that position, she reached across, carefully cleaning around the fan, wiping crumbs into the palm of her hand.

"Vince," growled Judith, "come' ere."

Vince waddled from the patio, huffed reluctantly up steps to the living room. He looked knackered. "What you want, woman?"

His wife explained Susan's predicament, Vince rubbed his groggy eyes with nicotine-stained fingers. "You got me up jus' t'tell me that?" and flopped down into the green settee. "The girl's prob'ly run outa gas. Hey, girl," he wheezed, delving for tobacco in the bowels of the pockets in his shorts, "d'yer bring any fence posts back wiv yer? Thought you mighta carried some back fer us. Shame," Vince joked, and gave Susan a critical eye. "When d'yer last fill up that tank?"

"Wyatt and I filled it last night."

"I wouldn't trust that Wyatt. You sure you filled 'im up?"

"Yes," replied Susan, "we emptied a drum into it, we syphoned fuel from the big drum."

"You sure? I mean I don't want to –"

"'Course she's sure," interrupted Judith, "she said she filled up that tank."

"Now don't you start," Vince churlishly rejoined, "don't you start gettin' at me, already got me up." The heat was affecting Judith and she was frustrated with her husband's querulous patter. She sat down in the reviving cross ventilation of the fan to thumb through a pile of crossword booklets on the grubby table. "I didn' get up to be got at by women," croaked Vince. "Where's me tobacco gawn?"

144

The couple often seemed to be subtly communicating across each other, rather than to each other, so the lines of their conversations became complex and competitive. Each time Vince thought he was winning, hot-blooded Judith, growing unpredictably angry, matched him with another point. Vince would run out of spunk, change his tune, and Judith become bored with her partner. Yet without fail, when Vince was absent, Judith uttered his name with affection.

"Where's me t'bacco gawn?" he grumbled.

Preoccupied, Judith ruminated. It was too hot to bicker; she sedated herself with a particularly flummoxing puzzle, select lashes covered her eyes.

"So 'ow long you take to walk back?" touted Vince and Susan had to retell her story. Judith butted in now, cheeping at how the couple had stopped, then driven on. "This is the outback, none o' yer genteel Poms 'ere. Git t'learn 'bout the bush, eh, Judith?" Judith flicked her attention back to the booklet, corners of the feather-weight pages twitching in the breeze.

Vince had no ambition to study and took pride in brashly announcing that he had been neither to England nor to university – believing the latter to be an exclusive international club, far from his idea of the realms of respectability, even more despicable to him than the class system. Vince revelled in insulting those who "'ad come out 'ere wiv their bleedin' qualifications an' degrees, degrees in what?" he'd scoff. "Degrees in bleedin' snobbery." He told Susan he had never met a British person who hadn't sub-scribed to this academic club; though that seemed incongruous to him because "what wiv Poms bein' prisoners of their country, 'ow the 'ell d'they get their bleedin' qualifications in the first place?" "You bin to university?"

Susan said she had studied drama at a college. "Don't know 'ow anyone can study drama. Mind you," Vince adjusted the cushions, "I've seen enough o' it in the yards, guess you could say I've studied drama too, eh?"

Susan piped up, "The vitality of the vernacular surpasses erudition."

Befuddled Vince was most effusive. "Couldn'a said it better meself."

"Maybe Susan is a real prisoner," figured Judith, looking up from her puzzle. "P'raps she 'as come 'ere to escape from somethin'."

"Ay, you a real prisoner from the mother country, eh? Ha, ha, ha. I know why them folks didn't stop, prob'ly thought she were bleedin' Abo or summin'. Eh, ha, ha!" Guffawing activated Vince's horrendous cough, tears streaked his cheeks though his eyes maintained the spry, nourishing look of the bush, which city people never acquire.

Resuming her study, Judith mumbled, "Shoulda stopped, eh, Vince?"

Vince relieved his lungs, hawking "did the job". "You best go t'bed, girl, 'ave a rest. Callum'll think we bin workin' you too 'ard."

"Come 'n' 'ave a coffee an' a smoke first," suggested Judith, heaving herself in the direction of the bunk-house kitchen. She looked askance at her uncouth husband and pointed a finger sculptured with age. "Tobacco's on the telly."

Susan slept well that night. When the first streak of day was in the sky she got up, dressed and braided her hair in front of her mirror. Little flies flew into the bunk-house on an early easterly breeze as she stepped into the corridor. The door to the end bedroom was slightly ajar. Seeing an oddly shaped heap lying on the floor, she paused. No one else appeared to be about. Susan stole across the corridor into the dawn lit room.

On the floor were dirty old stock saddles, leather cracked hard, wasted oil spoiled black, dusted in glittering sand; there was a kerosene lamp, hessian nose bags, mustering gear.

146

Davie had seen Susan come out of her room and slip through the open door. He was disturbed by the girl, followed her along the corridor and stood, secretly watching her body move.

Susan stooped beside the saddles, morning light from the window caught her hair. She had grown slimmer, browner and prettier each day. Davie noticed the things she was touching, the dusty saddles, the rope and gear. She seemed to lack all aggression. He scraped his thumbnail over the ginger stubble on his chin. She had mastered many new tasks; even when the vehicles had passed her on the roadside she did not respond. Davie knew how isolated Susan felt. He stepped forward, inarticulately seeking from her the kind of reassurance he used to be able to give.

Hearing his movement Susan looked round. Her sight was shifty. She wasn't sure what he was doing there, dressed up in silence. He came close to her, squatting low; vigorously he rubbed dirt from a saddle.

Susan sought a closeness in him, that old familiarity. Trusting still each move, she spoke. "Hello, Davie." Davie didn't speak at all. "Davie, what is it?" Susan asked. He looked at her, wanted her, his eyes searched her imploringly.

Susan looked away, afraid to look at him, partly because they had lost a closeness, partly because of Christine. Susan stood up and walked outside.

Davie was angry and hurt; their relationship felt fractured and repetitive, as though they kept failing the same hurdle. For her elusive ways, Davie despised Susan. She felt his rejection instantly.

She sat on the concrete steps of the bunk-house, rolling a cigarette. Grey galah perched on the washing line, the sky was blue, lightly clouded. On an intuitive level Susan understood what was happening between herself and Davie, though so much remained unsaid: there was an absence of possibility at the heart of their relationship, and both felt betrayed.

147

Davie trudged to and fro along the corridor; another relationship led nowhere and life's repetitions were a bore.

Feeling a strong allegiance with Christine, who clearly didn't trust Davie, Susan lit the cigarette. She wanted to find a home, was uncertain that this was the place. She watched white cloudlets passing by, and wondered how far she could travel and feel she was going nowhere.

She began to long for Callum. His presence. Back and forth Davie paced, Susan's thoughts ran from Callum to Davie. She shaded her eyes from the sun and looked back over the years; either this was some mysterious journey, or her life was a dreadful mistake she'd never quite learned how to face. Curious thoughts ran through her mind about Paddy and the black swans.

Susan slept in her room for an hour and was arranging frayed garments on her swag, her mind vacuous with a Dan Seals tape Callum had left in his pink cassette player, when she sensed company. It was Judith in the doorway.

"What that stuff you smell of? Always smell so sweet. That stuff you put in yer 'air?" Susan ejected the tape and showed Judith the supply of cream, a rich shade of ivory in a blue-topped tub. Judith dipped her nose into the receptacle and snorted, vociferating a full-throated moan. "Mmm, that's the stuff. 'N' that stuff you put on yer skin?" She trotted on, fascinated by a tall bottle in the small array of toiletries on top of the chest of drawers.

"Yes, it's cocoa butter."

"Smells nice too. May I?" Clucking maternally, Judith anointed her hands. "An' next time you're in town you can bring a crossword puzzle for me, eh?" Judith stroked the hair that, as a child, Susan had been so ashamed of. "'Eard you singin'."

Susan said, "I used to sing."

"Boab Festival's in a coupla weeks, you never bin, eh. If you can sing, you can sing at that festival, might win it. I'll be goin',

Da-vie, 'e'll be there." Judith always accentuated his name so it became drawn out. "Da-vie 'n' all that mob o' Hobson's." Bereaving Susan of her tender touch, Judith let locks fall. Susan was silent for a while. Judith wrinkled her brow, ushering something central between two women; one young, one old.

"What do you know about black swans?" asked Susan.

"Black swans?" Judith repeated, her eyes narrowed. "Southern bird. Kooljack, we call 'em 'long the Swan River. Each man, or boy, and girls of course, were given their totem. 'E woulda bin the totem for a clan. They were a source of food supply, protected. White fella thought they were unnatural, sum'ow."

"Did they have any traditional significance, the swans?"

The black swans were very significant. Judith felt disgruntled saying yes. "Each animal would have had a story – a story of the creation." Susan knew this and asked for the story of the swans.

"Paddy might tell you a thing or two. Nearly all the stories were lost."

"What does that make you feel?"

Inwardly Judith felt a strange homesickness she had thought she had pushed aside years ago, but it surfaced, and she sighed. "Sad. I feel sad 'bout that." Susan also felt sad – all meaning seemed to be lost, for the swans like the languages and people had dispersed.

Judith nodded knowingly. Goodness in the woman persisted, with this there was forbearance. She whispered, "You should enter that Country 'n' Western singin' competition at the festival in Derby next month. We'll all be there, the kids 'n' Vince an' me." Judith turned and walked back through the doorway.

There were two main kitchens: one in the homestead; one in a separate block with an open-plan dining room, a dry food store and a room with double metal sinks, three drainers and walls lined with white, meat-filled freezers. Then there was the

149

makeshift camp kitchen behind the bunk-house, plus Judith's barbecue and camp oven under the trees of the duck yard, backed by a fence with a beard of lilac and white striped flowers from the empire days. Here slugs of downy duck excrement masked the grass which Judith secreted daily with sand. Judith rarely cooked in the homestead kitchen, meal preparation was never fussy – the result, always tasty.

Every day wove an intricately delicate web of complications between Susan and Davie. Every day fragments of their relationship crumbled, disintegrating their rapport to a miserable debris. As Judith bustled in her matriarchal way, making the living room spick and span, Susan might help peel potatoes, carrots, pumpkins from the garden, chop onions, turn frying steak, or stir a simmering stew.

When the ringers stopped by for smoko, Judith and Susan rolled Log Cabin tobacco and joined them for a cuppa in the dining room. Down to the youngest of those cattlemen, Susan saw a bold quality, they were Australia's black heroes in bud.

All the men, except Vince and Davie's mob, ate together in the bunk-house kitchen; their tin mugs tarted the shelves. Mugs with chipped black rims, mugs of all sizes and colours: mint green, cream, red, old-white, each patented with a cattleman's signature inscribed into enamel.

A volatile hardness seemed to cast a pall over Davie. Wyatt was building the turkey so Judith's verve and consistently amicable spirit were merciful to the girl. Sensing Susan's anxiety, she would pop up sunny as a crocus and shrewdly attempt to console. "You come 'n' sleep in the main house wiv Vince 'n' me, there's a spare room, I'll make the bed up." Susan would be okay where she was. Or, "You got yer swag, 'ave a break from them boys." At lunch times Judith would whisper in Susan's ear, when Vince asked what she was saying she nudged Susan, teasing Vince with "women's secrets", she would not confess.

Amidst troops of tiny black ants parading on blue and white

150

linoleum, Susan camped in the spare room of the station house for one night. She missed Davie and Bushwhacker so much that she reverted back to the bunk-house the following evening, pining for Callum's return.

Davie's emotions pestered and sulked, platonic storm clouds begrudgingly dispersed, revealing a sultry electric eye – divine beauty oppressively moody – threatening thunder, tropical rain.

Along the gloomy corridor Susan strolled ruefully, watching Davie procrastinate, pulverising tobacco between his palms: he'd shift, share an unfinished smile, practise puffing phlegmatic smoke rings.

Susan lit a candle. The reclaimed, shadowy bedroom felt homely in the waxing conical glimmer balanced around the candle's wick. She lay on her bedding roll, waiting for the candle to burn itself out. Callum's dog shuffled a wet nose on to her swag. Clean, curled like a gipsy around Bushwhacker's systaltic, briar-haired body, she drifted asleep to the clock's tick-ticking.

Evening after evening in the dimly lit kitchen, lizards raced on white-washed walls and diligent Judith was captivated by cross-word puzzles – the gramarye of those booklets. Stocky Vince loafed, his profile turgidly chomping on his proceeds – a cold steak, his eyes tailored to the blank TV; or he lounged on the back veranda in a berth of inimical plastic chairs, to twiddle his thumbs and worry through debts.

Tense muscles relaxed when icy amber fluid soothed Vince's gullet, pre-empting his indelible cough. He would grouse and carp as he repeated an uninspiring epic for the hundredth time; his wife shut down her ears.

"Shout me a can," he habitually nagged her, "an Emu or Stubbie," from the hoard in the bilge of his cavernous deep freeze. Cans so cold they clipped lips, near froze fingertips; two were enough for the girl.

Wyatt was a loner. At night he lurked in his room. Behind the bunk-house Davie romanticised about rodeos 'n' horses 'n' this 'n' that to the ringers who burped and slurped by cooling coals in drunken darkness.

The stockman walked on colourless grasses that solemnly stirred under foot. The cool night air felt fresh about him as he floundered in the dark for his swag. Finding the bedding, Davie sat down, and set the can aside.

He thought of Callum, whose greatest strength was his kindness; the man was a bit of a rebel. To Callum little things mattered. " Listen," Callum had said, "I'm trying to say something." A supposition; Callum was being fastidious again. Run wild child, thought Davie, for ifs and buts are trite. Words, words drift through the moon. Words he spoke to himself.

Davie lay back on his bluey and breathed in the beauty of night. His avid eyes gazed: black on black on muslin Milky Way. He'd got news of Christine through the bush telegraph. He thought of her. Davie rolled on to his stomach. His other lovers never died, the ghost of them was deep inside. He wasn't getting any younger, nor was Christine. He wanted to awake with her there by his side.

Come sunrise he would head back to town. He'd go to a bar, then go see Christine. Nothing else was on his mind.

Road trains brought fresh cattle in the dark hours of the morning; wild short horn, long horn and horses finely bred. One truck dropped more ringers off, amongst them was Everette Owen.

Davie watched the young man walk across the yard, Everette Owen's form no more than a shadow on the sombre blue-black sky. The men talked outside the bunk-house. Everette Owen hated Davie for working with Susan. He felt betrayed, spoke with contempt, he'd lost two months' work to a girl.

152

"Why you bring 'er 'ere for, you wanna work with an English girl?" Owen laughed at Davie, who looked flustered, scratching his yellow hair. On and on they talked. The cockerel ceased his crowing, there was still no light in the sky. Davie, Everette said, was losing himself through the girl. Davie found the young man liberating and he himself wondered why Susan was there.

Owen walked to the yard and the cattle's heavy breathing, returning to the bunk-house at daybreak to choose himself a room.

Davie rolled his swag, deciding to stay, he carried the bedding back to his room.

Susan emerged from her room to the bunk-house corridor where Davie sat, moping on the floor in the doorway of his little bunk-house bedroom, profusely sullen, marring the arrival with his punitive retort.

"You gotta go back to town now." Susan asked him why. "What's wrong? Can't 'ear or summin'? Owen, 'e's 'ere, come 'ere t'work. Won't be needin' you no more, see," he indulged himself conceitedly, "yous gotta go back. Owen!" Forgetting the obstructive nature of his gauche paunch, clumsily Davie struggled to his feet, leant against the adjacent door, rapping on the veneer.

"Hey, Owen." He shoved the door open and entered. "Owen, she want to see you, she don't believe you're 'ere."

Everette Owen, a pallid, gangly youngster in new jeans and a black cotton shirt, sat on his bedding roll, primarily seeming quite meek. The room was semi-dark, bare; he didn't appear to have been doing anything. When he stood a hostile stature overlooked, hapless eyes scorned them from the addled face of the part-Aborigine; clothes hung on his spare rake of a body. Davie introduced Susan. Without a word, the youngster simply sidled back to his swag.

Davie's tone mellowed. "See, don't need you no more. Said you never shoulda come. You gotta go."

Davie's greeting at the breakfast camp was sour.

"Susan, you should do th' cookin'," kneeling his lustreless bulk on the soggy, trampled grass floor, his sallow pallor frostily reflecting the whey-faced dawn. Amidst charcoal chaff fluttering adrift, he grudgingly blew into the heart of a smouldering fire. With Owen he negated. "She should be cookin', eh."

Puffed, Davie rose, smeared grey ash smuts from unshaven cheeks down to the chest of his tartan shirt, and refuelled the fire with wood from the impoverished stack for the flicker to lick black. Sooty petals settled on Owen's head, sliding from glossy lank hair; he sat stonily on an upturned powdered milk tin of jumbo proportions, chin cupped in hands. Wyatt's mere presence visibly irked him. No one else spoke at breakfast. Wyatt moved, idly placing the makeshift oil drum stove over the flames, and they dolefully waited for the visage to heat. Each one solemnly fried their panful, turned toast, crouching close to the stove for warmth. The atmosphere grew increasingly repugnant.

Wyatt was first to leave. "I'll be takin' th' bug." Hatred drizzled out of Owen; he remained speechless. This change in Davie's character seemed too hurried to Susan. She felt like she needed to be with him through it somehow, to understand his point of view. She knelt up in wind-borne cinders, not sure whether to stay or go. Owen chastised with black opal eyes; Davie's timid face was sickly pale, steely eyes cyanic blue. Davie started. Susan froze.

Owen shouted, "Jus' fuck off! F 'in' bitch! I ain't workin' wi' th' bloody girl. You, Davie, you can 'ave 'er . Give 'er away. Jus' f'in' keep 'er outa my sight. F 'in' bitch. F' off!" Taking one hefty swing at the girl, he cruelly punched her forehead with a bony fist. A terrific thunderbolt came crashing down. A fearful darkness veiled her vision. It cleared as Owen, steaming, muttering obscenities, skulked round the corner of the bunk-house.

"I ain't workin' with th' f 'in' girl," bellowed Davie.

Susan had fallen, twisting an arm. She stumbled to the steps to sit down, feeling faint and very sick, shocked more by Davie than the blow.

That day Susan mourned, watching the dregs of Davie's kinship diminish and Owen's white hot anger. They were to replace the posts she had pulled up with a new line of fence.

"Get in that truck!" ordered Davie. Susan slunk into the back of the buggy in nervous anticipation. The men took her to a windmill on a solitary stretch of savannah, half-way between the station house and the end of the range, and left her there.

The world of want flooded back as an ancient world, new to Susan, retreated. She scrutinised the lichen's creamy frills carpeting the cracked concrete surround of the bore, dreaming, on this crude chair, that she could reach back through the torment of a dying closeness to salvage what had been. She wanted the work, this life, Davie, obsessively; scanning fallow grasses, she watched bitterly until the buggy had long disappeared.

Later he passed her by.

"What am I supposed to do?" Susan volunteered.

Venom oozed. "F'in' stay 'ere."

"What about water, Davie?" she hollered when he drove off. "You'll leave me some water."

"In the bore," he yelled back. "You can drink that f'in' bore!"

He couldn't call me a lover, she said to herself, I've never treated him that badly – guess I've always blown against the wind. But I'm here still, and I want to be like this always: free in the open expanse of exile, for cloisters, a discerning peripheral range. Swirling, twirling desolate freedom. Free with the plain, the sky, the horizon. Free from advice. Free with hushed grasses waving. Free to feel the greatest freedom of all: solidarity in being solitary – not from folk, from strife and insanity, the claustrophobic comfort of material life.

Davie and Owen eventually picked her up, forging through the hottest part of the day, they took her to the bunk-house where

Bushwhacker's emphatic greeting, his tail working energetically, was of that innocent over-eagerness only dogs possess.

She used to sing when every day was vital – like being in love: watching the cherry blossom dripping, taking time to smell the flowers. Yet in thinking back she shudders. Who wouldn't? The audacity. They tried to stop the flow. Had she not the choice to do with or without? Evidently not. So it's hardly surprising that she'll never travel light now. Perhaps never has. Expect no light relief, no short cuts. For years she held back and when she was prepared to let it out, she lost the way.

She used to sing. But after she found them reading her life ... Imagine that. Burning all of her diaries. Diaries written throughout her teens. Seven years. The key to the map. Seven. A lucky-for-some-number burnt in fury. The map quite gone. So she'll never really know. One can guess. She knows there's a place she'll never find, and that she'll never know again quite how it felt in '76. The sizzling summer fever. Itchy-scratching. Fervent cider, boldly swigging adolescent, enjoying the thrill of her impending absence, drinking the season away. Hazily remember, sure. Drowsily she remembers the ditch at the far end of the field. Her favourite ditch.

She didn't drink or smoke at home. Not until "Mum" caught her with a fag end in her hand. Sitting up in bed, the butt behind, burning the pillow. She denied it even then. Because she was so horrible, an ugly duckling discarding school, "Mum" said she was one drink under – took her to three shrinks. But she'd always been afraid of the dark. Deep water and the dark. When the maze of dreams had themes, hidden behind the cupboard's deep, dark doors, safe within its fathomly drawers, lay bottles and bottles of sunshine then.

She'd never got as close as she did that first time, cider beside. Repeatedly playing the same old tracks: "Here Comes The Sun", "Only The Good Die Young". She wanted to be one of them, little darlin'. Dead, not good. The hues drift in and the balms waft by. The suicide stench lingers.

She used to sing.

156

Alone Davie drove out to the spinifex plain and the coralline mountain range. Owen went to his room. Susan plodded towards the homestead where one of the blue dogs was snooping around below the wooden steps in a gloomy mulch of feathered duck excrement. As Susan approached, the dog raced out, leaping up, snapped at her arm. Judith must have heard the cry, she tore out of the kitchen, in one fell swoop thumped the heeler and caught hold of the arm Susan nursed.

"He's drawn blood?" Judith asked hurriedly.

Susan shook her head. "It's bruised, that's all."

Sheltered by trees scorched from the dry, Judith observed Susan's face with a far-sighted look. "I never 'ad kids o' me own, just looked after 'em, big mob." Ducks gabbled by the garden fence wreathed in neglected colonial flowers. Judith took Susan under her wing; her warm black arms were chequered in shade. "I looked after them kids they took from their fam'lies, 'alf-castes taken from wailin' girls an' put in cities or brought up in church missions. I looked after some 'oo escaped."

A breeze rustled the leaves of the trees, shedding light obliquely so the strain of remembrance showed in Judith's face. She merged Susan into cordial creases. There was compassion in her voice, unlatching a window to her heart. "Even split up sisters 'cos their eyes were different shades. Some o' them kids didn' know where they'd come from, or where to go. I know 'ow they felt 'cos they split up my family too. I was from the coastal people, lived out near the estuary."

In strong arms caressing, warm arms wrapping her into a purple pinafore dress, as the black swan mothers a native young, Judith drew the youngster to a resilient breast.

Susan's throat went tight, she wanted to leave the past behind, but it kept coming up from the lawn where hearts had screamed for long-lost mothers, and unleaked grief was atoned. With the whispering leaves she heard the voice of a child, removed from her mother; it was a muffled cry. It was her own cry, filled with

157

confusion in rooms filled with noise; everyone was talking at once, the child's cry had become muted by the prejudices of those around her. They impeached all measure of contentment. Susan saw the child so pained with invisible demons tossing her into rapids of misunderstanding, that she had ceased feigning feeling part of the family.

Angry flames plagued Susan's heart. In Judith came no evil, she was binding them together, closing out the careless world. "Them politicians took all them kids from their parents right up till recently, said it would be best for future generations that way, but it's no good for the kids an' parents 'oo's alive now, an' 'oo's to say there was anythin' wrong with the Aboriginal way?"

They stood in silence.

Beneath the trees' impartial darkness, their painful past came gnawing back as they floated, impressionistic, in childhood recollections. Susan clenched her eyes shut when memories rushed through her mind: she was in her early teens, somehow searching for answers, had revolted against being the social misfit with unpredictable tantrums which angered her adopted parents to such an extent, they beat her. Each thump felt as though they were crushing the black voice inside of her; she had painted her bedroom brown in the vague hope that this might protect it, but such efforts were whitewashed over, and Susan was ordered out of the house. It was a downward spiral, escalating her sense of isolation.

Having found and faced such grief, Susan was left with a dull ache in her belly. She opened her eyes and looked at Judith's perceptive face. More in sorrow than in anger she cut short what had passed. Though pathos had been in her words, Judith knew forgiveness was reconciliatory, releasing the girl from her arms. Ducks' tails waggled as they proudly puffed up plumage. Judith led Susan back to the homestead, the grass felt coarse between their toes.

Nightfall came quickly. Susan sat in her room on her swag, mending a ragged shirt by candlelight. She was quite distressed, most of her clothes were in tatters and everything seemed too incomplete, too much a mirror of before. Once again she had found work, once again the situation was falling apart. Night noises from the scrub carried into the bunkhouse. Susan peered up at the little window. It was pitch black outside. She went back to her sewing, darned her clothes as best she could as dancing shadows lengthened. But she was tired, deeply disillusioned with Davie. The most painful times were randomly placed. Unfairly spaced. Desperate for a sense of belonging, Susan began to cry.

She heard the wind in the trees and the voices she had heard before in the leaves. Voices of the past. The sound streamed into the room, full of sorrow. Millions of voices, stemming from injustice – the disorders of the dispossessed raging round the world became one mournful cry, defying all sense of time. A wonderful resonant sound, powerful and passionate. Though the path seemed hard and dark, Susan's voice became one of many.

Her eyes washed clear with tears, all that had been, all that she had thought she had wanted didn't seem so much to matter. Then Susan felt peace, mysteriously. She blew the candle out, falling into a deep sleep.

Vince shot a killer early the next day. Strewn with eucalyptus branches, it bounced back to Sun Creek in his truck. He was butchering the beast on the front lawn, hacking at the top flank, whilst Judith, under the trees of the duck yard, stooped to light the barbecue fire. Chuffing in the wood smoke, Vince slung enormous rib bones into an eski. Judith helped pile steaks on wire mesh bed frames outside the bunk-house

159

kitchen, divided and tidied choice pieces into plastic bags for freezing; scrounging dogs and hunks of beef seething with flies dotted the garden. Susan appeared to watch Judith boil the brawny textured tongue in a cauldron.

Placing himself on a chair nearby, watery-eyed Vince savoured the pungent aroma of tobacco in his tin. "What 'bout this ol' goanna, Susan," slurred Vince, "we call 'im bar-ni, when you gonna catch 'im?"

Susan was a little shy. "I don't know how to catch a goanna. I've never done that."

"Jus' find 'im 'n' jump on 'im," said Judith. "Jump on 'is back, 'old 'im down, tie 'im up an' I'll 'elp you bring 'im in. I'm too old t'catch 'im, 'e move too fast. I'll come wiv you to that dump, we'll take Bushwhacker, 'e'll track 'im. We can go now if y'like."

Susan readily agreed. Vince supplied Judith with a bight of plastic rope, Susan roused Bushwhacker: the hunting party was complete.

A council of cattle by the disused corral, grazing hindered by the harsh heat, gazed reflectively as Judith and Susan passed. Bushwhacker jogged alongside Judith who skirled at Freezer and Blackarse until their retreat. The cows' stench spread across uneven, sandy bush land on the far side of the enclosures, following the couple to the dump.

Distorted fence posts jutted like jack-straws from cranky cars mounting mangled wrecks of rusted trucks that had sunk in a rotting debris of corrugated cardboard and goodness knows what, from which erect trusses of wind-grass sprouted. Intermittent strips of spinifex broken by spruce meetings of gum and eucalyptus saplings partitioned the numerous metallic mounds. It was very hot.

Judith and Susan waded knee-high in spinifex, wound round beastly labyrinths, precarious and inorganic. Keeping a sharp lookout, Judith halted to rerun through her plan. "When we find 'im, you jus' run-'n'-jump-on-'is-back, 'old 'im down then 'e can't scratch you or git you wiv 'is tail, an' I'll come 'n 'elp 'old the old bugger. Then we'll tie 'im up wi' this rope an' take 'im back. Vince'll kill 'im."

Susan wasn't convinced about jumpin' on 'im, but then she had never seen 'im.

In front of them, supporting the ruined body of a car, was the crumpled cab of a rusted truck. "'E could be in one o' them piles." Judith approached the heap of vehicles: in a gallery the construction of convoluted metal might have passed as a work of art, here it was just a gratuitous jumble, remnants of better days.

Judith peered into the glassless cab's window. "We can poke 'im out." She vigorously extracted two buckled fence posts wedged between the battered cab and a bald tyre, the flagging wreckage groaned. Encouraging Susan to probe into the dark shell of the cab, Judith clattered her lance against decaying iron to no avail, then set off thrashing through glistening spinifex to another pile. "You jus' jump on 'im an' I'll 'elp you 'old 'im down. Bushwhacker could've killed 'im if 'e wasn't so big 'n' tough."

The more Judith wagged, the greater Susan's vision of this creature became, the less she actually wanted 'im to appear and the less sure she was that she would want to jump on 'im if 'e did. Bushwhacker's random scaremonger tactics, directed solely at alarming fowls of the air instead of tracking down the intended prey, appeared highly suspect; Susan couldn't help feeling he might continue to employ these capricious tactics should the ultimate moment arise.

Judith looked around adversely. "Well, I don't know where 'e's gawn. 'E usually 'bout 'ere somewhere."

Susan queried the woman on the goanna's size. "How big is it?"

"Dunno. 'E's bin 'ere so long 'e could've died. 'E'll be tough to eat. Old one that goanna. 'E about this long," estimated Judith, stretching her arms wide, "'bout four," wider, "me'be five foot.

'E's a big one. You betta watch out, you mustn't let that bar-ni get you with 'is tail. Knock y'down, 'e can whack y'down with 'is tail, break yer legs. You be careful, if 'e sees you out in the open 'e might think you're a tree 'n' run up yer."

"Oh."

"Watch out f'snakes 'ere in th' tall grass," cautioned Judith, scything for the reptile.

"Judith, I've never caught a goanna, I'm not so sure I can."

"Nah," neighed Judith, "nah, you'll be right, I used to catch 'em as a kid. Jus' gotta be quick. Don't think twice when you see 'im, jus' go-'n'-jump, then 'e can't scratch you or git you with 'is claws," she flexed her fingers predeterminately. "'E'll 'ave big claws this one."

Armed with fence posts, they rattled and rooted in decomposed scrap and agitated spinifex, Judith repeatedly advising Susan to watch out for snakes or the old goanna in case 'e jumped outa that pile, while Bushwhacker had a wonderful time, bouncing through the hip-high grasses, chasing tiny bush birds into flight.

"Ha! Found 'is tracks 'ere all over the place. 'E might be 'ere, but these could be old tracks too. See 'is tracks?" Distinctly marking the red sand were the footprints of a gigantic lizard, etched between them, a heavy line: "That's where 'is tail sweeps the floor." The tracks were really quite beautiful: patterns resembling images Susan had seen in local paintings. They led in and out of the saplings to another inane waste heap which Judith examined and disturbed periodically with her stick, while Susan squinted at the sun's brightness, waiting with bated breath for the monster to dart out.

Bushwhacker yelped, they looked up and there, on the far side of the dump, near where they had entered, was the rogue. It looked hideous to the girl; a brutal dragon. She was so relieved when Judith caterwauled.

"'E's seen us! 'E's seen us!" No sooner had Judith started

braying when the old goanna turned tail for cover. "That no good. No good jumpin' on 'im, 'e run 'way too fast. Bushwhacker, 'e might bring 'im round." The dog immediately bounded in the opposite direction, joyfully barking, leaping and snapping at rising green parrots and snowy galahs.

"We'll come back another day," said Judith despondently. She looked very disappointed and foiled, then smiled with a determination that indicated that their efforts were not thwarted. "Well, at least we know 'e's still 'ere."

Susan assumed that their drunken orgies accounted for a deflated Davie and Owen each breakfast. One morning Vince said Davie was to complete missing links in the new fence line, he asked Susan to assist him.

"Can do that on me own," Davie bleated impotently. "She best cookin' wiv Judie."

"Git on with it, ya bastard," sanctioned the manager, "'n' take the girl wiv yer, you'll be quicker that way. Owen 'n' me'll 'elp Wyatt up at that turkey, then tomorrow you can all work at the turkey, puttin' in the new fence round 'er."

The stubble had grown on Davie's face in the brief period since he and Susan last worked together, and his kinship was frail. They didn't work in unison. There was no sunshine, the stagnant air was flooded with flies and a fog of black bees.

It took the whole day to string sheets of corrugated iron over the dry creek beds, thus preventing cattle from straying below the wire.

Pioneering through unbroken bush the stockman hewed ahead. Swaggering up steep gravel banks, dislodging swarf, sand glissading from his boots, he harnessed a strand of barbed wire to a tree on the cusp of the bank where the new fence ended, lobbed the remainder of the roll to the far side, tumbled back down the slope face and blustered up scree opposite to reef in the strand

163

and marry it where the new fence began again. He tightened the slack of the runner by hand, wrenching it taut with a strainer.

Susan had forgotten her gauntlets and got a splinter as she bumbled through hazardous undergrowth after Davie.

Heavy-handed, hobbling as he toiled, Davie bashed holes at one end of a rectangular sheet with a mallet; he clobbered Susan with a keen metal spike and scathed her injured arm. Then he and Susan crashed, clashing unmanageable sheets of iron with fragile, rusted corners.

"Do yer bit then," glowered Davie. His eyes challenged hell's fire. Anarchic flies swarmed.

Susan held the sheets high in the air, long-ways down, the brittle tops buckled and fractured as Davie forced wire loops through holes and spliced them round the runner strung across the bank. He winched the corrugated sheets up until they swung like iron curtains, low enough from the creek bed to prevent cattle from walking below.

Davie stepped back to give the installation a rapid survey in an infuriating mist of flies. "Should be right," he said with a second glance, "till the rains anyways, then they'll all get washed away."

Susan asked him why he'd let her come if he didn't want her there.

"Come where?" he hissed.

"Here, to Sun Creek, after I rang you in Derby."

"Couldn't jus' leave you," he shrugged at the yoke of his onerous burdens. "What was I s'pposed to do? Couldn' jus' leave you there." he swatted flies feasting on his face. "Man shouldn' do things like that, jus' leave a woman. See, you don't know this country, me, 'ere I know my way 'round."

Impulsively swiping at insatiable insects, Davie blethered, "These fuckin' flies! This ain't no way to work. A man can't work. I can't do dis, can't think with these damn flies up everywhere!" Shaking his head hysterically, sweat on his brow, dust in his hair, his fingers in and out of ears.

Davie's consternation was exacerbated by flies. It was as though life's prolonged agonies permitted pests to fester in a head of frustrations and rankle the brain cancerous. Susan watched with frightened eyes.

Stamping in torment he walloped a tree, then his cheeks reddened and flamed. "Drivin' me bleedin' crazy you, that's what," squealed Davie. "Gonna drive me crazy, crazy this work. You'll be right, you'll jus' go off, f ' off back to England, me, I'm stuck wiv it!"

Embers of the fire Susan had lit for smoko smouldered on the stony creek bottom. In the pile of unused kindling was a eucalyptus branch, vestured in parchment leaves. Davie ignited these leaves, in sunless humidity, under leaden skies, took manic strides up the briary bank, flailing the forked flambeau through a blizzard of flies and the hackle of undergrowth. The branch was touchwood to the leaves of a eucalyptus on the cusp; before long the famished tree was a rush light, then a roaring blaze.

Inwardly Susan was horrified, silently pleaded with her eyes, took one last look, turned and fled from the creek bed, her heart beating to the rhythm of what Davie bore; scrambling desperately up the bank, each thud drumming through her ears, she ran out to open spinifex plain.

Tragically edged by a scrawny thicket the raving stockman raged, "Gonna kill this bleedin' place right 'ere. Gonna kill 'em flies. It's me or them!"

A symbolistic change manifested in the way Davie treated Susan after he set fire to the scrub. He had been so cantankerous, had always been abrupt; he remained ruffled, shrouded by a flaring beacon haloed in black smoke twisting, blistering open country, but his stormy stare became less jaded; his vengeful wrath was vanquished.

A car door slammed. From the darkness a voice rang out. "My shout this little lot." It was Callum back from Derby, provisions piled high in the yellow pick-up. He was slimmer, spruced up in a new black shirt, black hat and dark glasses. When the bubbly commotion his arrival evoked had settled, still grinning, he flounced over to Susan.

"Jude say y'missed me." He beamed his air of well-being. "One minute," and fetched a beer: with a perceptible spring in his gait and fresh can in hand, Callum breezed along the bunk-house corridor, making a seat, one rise above Susan, on the steps.

The clouded night was cold with only a few stars. High-pitched and strident was the cicadas' stipulating hum in the air, glow worms shone in the grass around the bushes where Judith had been cooking.

"How was Derby?" Susan asked.

"Never like bein' in town too long, takes summin'." Callum's mellifluous lilt recapitulated his anecdote of Pigeon's story – words bounced off his tongue. "No pleasin' me with them material things – not f'long any rate. Ain't right bein' there more 'n a day or two. Vince said you work well, surprised me y'know, but we finished 'ere. Be drivin' yous all back t'Derby in a coupla days."

Susan felt unworthy of Callum's praise, and silly talking to her reflection in the breaker's shades as she tried to explain the shambles that had occurred while he was away. "We had a disagreement, an argument, Davie, Owen and me. They say they won't work with a girl, so I helped Judith."

Callum attacked the pull-ring, swigged his nectar, smacked his lips and demurely deepened his tone. "I'll talk t'Davie 'bout it, 'bout what you said. 'E treat you bad?"

"Kind of."

"That's no good. Why you think 'im treat you bad? Thought yous were good mates, eh?" Callum removed his dark glasses.

"Yeah," sniffled Susan, "we were. Well, we are, I still like Davie

166

– it was Owen. He, well he … and Davie just copies him." Her eyes turned to Callum. He looked exasperated, casting his gaze to the night sky, then, auburn lids lowering, focused on a frivolous party of moths, confetti about their heads. Like the little stars, a glint flitted in his childlike eyes. He swiped at a silver-thistledown creature, milling powdery wings, the remnants lightly fell in the grass.

"What did Owen do? You cryin'?" inquired Callum, unable to disguise his disappointment. Lamenting, relinquishing the walls of discontent built since his departure, Susan's malaise gave way to tears. She rested her head on her knee to hide their flow.

The cicadas succinctly quit their chirping. The breaker let time elapse.

"Davie hurt you?"

Susan tried to say, "Only inside," but words didn't come. Just wretched, crestfallen tears.

A warm hand caressed her neck, spreading over the nape, intimately soothing, dispelling sorrow. She was mesmerised by the slow way he rocked, peace overpowered speech, silence reigned. The hand tenderly massaging the bare nape spanned so close to her ears that she could hear and feel it in synchronism.

"He hurt you, eh?" Susan didn't want Callum to talk: she felt as though an upside-down world had caved in, all that was left was the comfort of the hand and the body it extended from. "What then?" he tentatively urged, fondling her neck with painstaking care.

"It's not Davie …" When she discovered a voice, words seemed inconsequential. "They didn't … didn't mean harm."

"Did he hurt you? Hey, Susan, did he hurt you?" The condemnation of a confused failure swept over Susan, congealed by the man's sensuous touch. "Hey, don't cry now. Don't cry. You jus' tell me what happened." Callum cared so much in that moment that Susan felt she could burst. She prayed for him to never lose his sensitivity, to be this way always.

The steps were cold. They sat together, absorbed. The carnal warmth from the man's open palm tacitly healing, whispering.

"You right?" Susan nodded. "Wanna see Judith?"

"No, I'm all right."

"Okay now?" He rubbed deep into the blades of her shoulders, his thumb nurtured her spine, eased off and let go. Even when he didn't touch her physically his tenderness was there, all night, reaching her heart, holding it together.

"Yeah, well, Owen, 'e's only a boy, 'e don't know what it was like in them ol' days see, when we all used t'work together on these stations, women 'n' children 'n' all. 'E not used t'workin' with women, jus' worked with men, see, 'e don't know." Callum said it was okay, pinched Susan's shoulder and she knew he was right.

He sipped at the beer. "Worse things 'ave 'appened, eh? An' Davie, 'e should know better. Bushwhacker says 'e kept you company, eh? We'll all be goin' back soon anyways an' I'll be layin' all of you off. I gotta go north fer a bit, finish off some fummin' fence I started way back, got some colts t'break at the plot I got in Derby too. But I'll talk wiv 'em, Davie 'n' Owen, they shouldn'a treat you bad.

"Vince say you bin workin' miracles, pulled up more of 'em posts in one day than anyone an' then more the next day. This true? So you like fencin'? Beats cricket, eh? Hey girl," Callum purred, "all good things come around, come t'gether again. Gonna give a smile?"

Susan looked round and smiled straight at him. They stood, stretched and returned to their rooms.

The oranges didn't appear but Callum had stocked up with vegetables, tobacco, beer, and the following morning, in the corridor outside Susan's bedroom door, lay a spotless pair of white cotton gauntlets, leather palms scrupulously doubled in.

168

The last day flew by. Everette Owen with his maverick bearing played truant, Callum was in the pink of condition. He and Susan cut scaffolding poles, dug holes and soldered gates. The gauntlets he had brought from Derby were in shreds when they twinned fence posts with wire at the new turkey fence.

In the balmy flamingo evening light on grasses of the plains, dust puffed gold about their ankles and Callum was more debonair than ever; the setting sun rayed from the breaker's smile. Even his rebuke was frolicsome when he reprimanded Wyatt, whose labours had resulted in a skewiff turkey.

Callum cried: "*Snake*!"

Davie jumped: "Where?" The old joke elicited the desired response and they all laughed together at non-existent reptiles in the grass.

The splinter Susan had got while working with Davie hindered her; as the magnolia twilight bedimmed, she sat in the bunkhouse corridor, trying to dig the brute out with a needle. Davie tripped on her foot, Susan drew her legs in.

"Nah, you're right. Hey, what yer up to?" he asked auspiciously. "Come 'ere then, lemme see." Davie sat down at Susan's side, she pointed to the thorn. "Can't see nothin'."

"It's big as a tree, Davie, look."

Davie took her thumb. "Still can't see. Oh yeah. Hey, Callum, girl's got a splinter."

Callum squatted at her other side. "Lemme see." The thorn throbbed horribly, it was embedded in a red bulge. "You got summin' to get 'im out with?"

"Yeah," said Davie, "she bin pickin' at it fer ages."

Callum examined her thumb in diffracted light. "How long've you 'ad that mongrel there?"

"Callum'll get it out," said Davie. "You'll get 'im out for 'er, eh?"

"Best take it out," Callum was half asking, half stating. "You

169

wanna 'ave me get it out, eh?" Susan nodded. Callum clamped her hand between his knees. "Gi'me the needle, an' look th' other way."

Sifting through broken dreams, Davie stood, looking at Susan. "Gi'me the jitters, I'm gettin' a beer."

Tranquillity contained Callum's movements, he nipped the tip of Susan's thumb between a thumb and forefinger and, with single-minded regard, mulled over the pores of her skin. Barely daring to breathe, so pure was his observance, Callum used his sharp eyes and the needle that pricked the print of her thumb.

The smell of his flesh was fresh from showering. Gratified by the alert man's undivided intent, Susan studied his calmed features, so carefully carved and coloured brown.

"Yo, you're lookin'," he crooned. Words didn't follow her disposition – there was so much to thank the man for – all this was soon to end.

Susan felt a twinge, Callum drew the speck out, she winced, grimacing at hurtful things for want of expression. Still clasping her thumb with one hand, Callum held the splinter up to view. He just said, "That's a-son-ov-a-bitch."

Darkness doused the sky. Davie, by the heap of reclaimed fence posts, packed their gear into the pick-up. Wyatt stood aloof at the entrance to the bunk-house corridor as a full moon rose, outlining his wiry form.

In her bedroom Susan sat with a candle on the linoleum floor, and closed her eyes for recollecting, imagining England: walking along Plymouth's streets, these she saw as equivocal corridors crammed with arcades promising everything. Saturday shoppers, pushchairs galore; she felt walled in by tower blocks closing, bricks obliterating the sky. Visualised meticulous lawns mown to an inch, where any wild plant was a weed; the foibles of the country folk now seemed petty, the Cornish valley she had once enjoyed, twee, and with her stockmen, no one compared.

Susan heard Davie laugh, opened her eyes and went to look

out of the window. Moonlight streamed through the gauze, lighting her cheek with softness. She placed her hands either side of the tiny window frame, her chest against the sill, gazing out at night sky; an expansive space. It was like *being* in the middle of space. Living there, working on a fence line in the wilderness. A few distant stars twinkling. Old stars. Old dreams. She knew them, reached for them in ancient hills floating in infinity. A strange place. A dot, working her way back; scarred by wire, gorged by sounds full of emptiness. And those flies pestering her, Davie bothering her. If it wasn't one it was the other, hoping they would get her to lie down.

Susan left her room for the bunk-house corridor, where moonlight flowed on concrete. She sat down on a step in the penumbra of eaves and saw another side to the men, now the day was over and they knew they'd worked their best.

By the camp oven, under the trees of the duck yard, the sleeping garden was broken by firelight, where the men drank, where stories start. Yarns about horses, rodeos and bully bulls. No vainglory, hats still on, a tape of country music playing.

Susan's hands were rough as sandpaper. The past and future felt so far; she wanted to hold each moment as though it were the last and wished she could share this forever. Easy time. Evening time. Time to spare. Davie and Callum laughing, heads back, eyes closed, composed silhouettes lazily breathing. The scene was like music. The scene was the music portraying the dilatory scene. Bitter sweet wood smoke, shadows tall in darkness, kind hearts and laughter welcoming the night.

Callum doffed his hat, his voice pattered like faraway horses' hooves, bringing back the old days, his first rodeo, the stock camp at Fitzroy.

The firelight waned. It was cool. They spoke in whispers. A cattle truck was approaching, she heard it rumble through the mountains.

Tammy Wynette sang long and sad. Davie fell asleep. The

171

tape was playing "One Day At A Time". Davie, beached up like a huge whale on canvas, was snoring, over there, on his swag. And the tape was playing "There Goes My Reason For Living".

In her head Susan could hear those bees buzzing, the generator, the cattle bellowed in the yard. A dingo howled in the bush and she looked to the moon. The tape was singing "Only The Lonely" to itself. Those times. Those men ...

It was a fair, clear sky, stars hung soft and sharp. Callum and Susan, quenched by vivacious constellations, counted shooting planets dive as they sat by termite tombs in the dirt of the track side, waiting for the others. He gave her the unexpected – secureness in the darkness; as her true father had given to her that unpredictable island and gave her to drink a warm sea breeze, the sensuous fragrance of honey, salty tasting of fresh white waves that hound the sandy bay's shore. The breaker's eyes were jewels emerging, they were aroused by night travelling. "We call 'em the emu. See that emu in the sky?" Callum painted past the Milky Way to a multitude of starry galaxies. The scrub was raw with the night's inclemency, their inner warmth flowered.

Blinding headlights floodlit the path for the buggy bombarding towards them. Davie, carousing on whisky, stood on the passenger seat between Owen and Wyatt, he yodelled and wassailed, brandishing his bottle, swearing as he reeled over bumps in the track, shirt billowing behind.

"What happened to you mongrels? Thought yous were gonna tail us," reprimanded Callum, but the unbridled gang were too far gone to have a care. They dropped behind and caught up again, their main beam dazzling in the pick-up's rear view mirror all the way to town.

They slept by the road on the outskirts of Derby. Birds sang righteously as the sun broke through and they left the buggy to filter into the pick-up with haphazard bundles of goods and chattels.

Callum deposited Owen near the water tower, pulling up opposite the rodeo grounds for Wyatt and Davie to unload their blueys. Wyatt waved. Davie didn't say goodbye. Susan passed him alongside the white poles of an enclosure, their heads turned in an inadequate silence. She hadn't seen him since that sunrise in the reddened rodeo grounds when, eucalyptus black against a gold sky, he grabbed her; violet-blue eyes piercing, swollen face ruddy, belly chubby, full of beer. He was all dust and shrouded in shafts of sunlight – her heart was drawn to him. They retained a kindred spirit, the hurt for what they had never had remained.

Callum helped Susan across the road with her swag. He said he hoped they would meet again, cocked his head happy-go-lucky, fashioned the sweep on his black hat's rim and sauntered back to his faithful truck.

Susan hired a jeep and drove away from Derby. When the outskirts of town were broken by bush, buff grasses whittled away to scrub, scorched brown, and the straight highway stretched ahead. A long curve uphill, a long curve down, each peak unfolding a trough, another band of highway.

Either side of the road was a white line, either side of the line, small stones sprinkled a ribbon of red dust. Sometimes the monotony was split by the slender, silvery-white body of a eucalyptus, sometimes solitary black stumps. Inlaid with stones, the bitumen reflected the spectrum colours, sparkling like priceless jewels. Red dust glittered, and in the white dust and scrub near the roadside, broken bottles glinted, winking throughout the day.

Stretching on before Susan, the road was like a line between past and future along which she was moving. Sometimes the scrub opened into grassy expanses of green, yellow patches of grasses, or the bushes were taller, thicker. Memories came flood-

173

ing back as eddies of dust whirled, weightlessly teasing and raising red dirt that lay behind. Hot sun kisses softened the road leaving a blurred, shining reflection running alongside the jeep. Sky-blue sky melted into pale blue, getting whiter, lighter, mixing a few strokes of bright white cloud growing into a sea.

Susan looked to the future for hope when evening light lined bushes, and the luminance at sundown was spectacular, each cloudy sheet sparked with a resplendent celestial wash. Then she saw her aspirations lead back to herself.

Small white posts marked one hundred yards of highway; white reflectors on the right, red reflectors left. Glowing fiery red edges illuminated either side of the road, as the earth breathed in the dying sun, the night exhaled a moon.

Susan had bleary-eyed memories of stopping in the smallest hours, stumbling from the jeep to cold blackness, blundering across a void of tarmac towards the yellow neon signs of a road house; icy air friezed the moon and stars about her head. Gripping a smooth, yellow plastic rail in a sluggish, disoriented queue; the greedy amber glow of bacony men, red-necked farmers of the "deep north" joining truckers tucking into chicken nuggets and fillet 'o' fish. Hands warmed when supping steaming sweet tea from a white ceramic mug, eyes closed, head drooping; a change of scene, a break in the journey and all Susan wanted was a cigarette and a whole lot more out of life. The restaurant cleared. Susan stood with others wearily, in preparation for the shock of night-chilled darkness and walking, ankles cut with cold, to realise she had no idea where the jeep was. "Oh God, it's been stolen. Who cares." She was too tired when she fumbled on board, hearing the radio, feeling the warmth she noticed when buses glided by. Then it was Susan that drifted – on the move again. The familiar hum, the familiar drum, the drizzle of sounds as she sailed through night, mesmerised by rushing country by day.

Apart from all the broken glass, there wasn't much roadside litter. A bundle of tape, torn strips weathered, loosely decorated

174

a tree, like tinsel, it caught the transient light. Susan cruised along Darwin's deserted streets, heading for the airport between sombre, low-rise blocks of the downbeat urban sprawl.

After parking the jeep, lumbering with a multitude of bags to be weighed, checked in, forestalling at the bar, and all the other mundane procedures she went through when travelling alone by air, her preoccupation grew, and with it, the desire to return. To go home. Where was home?

Her eyes settled on a sign: "International Airport". The words conjure up images of wide departure lounges, long, luxurious settees, modern decor, an ambience of draughty detachment. Although it scheduled flights all over the world, that is not how Susan saw Darwin airport in 1990 – a poky, shabby hangar; air-conditioning cooled that humid afternoon. A stark contrast to the bright sunlight that left her blinkered on entering such a dreary, lightless building.

Craving Davie's company, she wrote to him and rang. In those agitated tones she could hear the horses' hooves, the stockman's murmur; "I'll do that one day, take you off a galloping horse"; smell the red dust, the heat; see the moon at least for a moment in quivering grasses, she was back there, with them.

There was a rush of warm air as automatic doors slid apart to release the throng of passengers, crossing concrete in shimmering heat before mounting the metal-runged ladder. Every moment seemed delayed, welcoming gestures from the crew, prolonged; after safety belts were secured and the safety demonstration completed in an absurd, ritualistically slick, self-conscious manner, the majestic machine was in motion. The plane turned, gently reversed, framing scenery by small, smoothly moulded, white-ledged windows. Then she swung round and was runway rolling to gradually gather speed. The steady build of noise and power increased with acceleration and the immense urge inside Susan equalled the surge of engine roar. Faster. Panic. Faster. Chaos. Tearing tarmac, welling tears. Outside, low-lying bush,

175

brown bristled grass a blur; inside, an iron stomach and an overwhelming compulsion lodged innermost. The rise in determination to return to the Kimberley coincided with the exhilaration of lift-off. Throat tight, ears blocked, freedom from the ground. Sea-blue. Sky-blue.

Up in the air she sat, unnerved by such a long flight. Where was the woman who worked with the men, looked them in the eye; kindly, carefully, gently said no; softly meant no. Laughed with them. That happiness now seemed so short-lived, though she would – if she could – have stayed there. Susan had lost the path ... to succeed she had to start again. Start what again? Start where? The sky outside became dark. Scared of the emptiness around her, Susan felt that hope was dying. A glimpse was enough to let her remember what she should have had. But the more she understood, the faster it slipped away. Blindness crept back. She could feel herself falling. Didn't think she had the energy to climb; and although she had striven to be free from this her home was that of the homeless, in a passage between, with faraway stars on the other side of the glass.